The Imaginary Plays

Spain
Saltimbanques
Green Man

Jim Knable

A SAMUEL FRENCH ACTING EDITION

SAMUEL FRENCH

FOUNDED 1830

SAMUELFRENCH.COM
SAMUELFRENCH-LONDON.CO.UK

FOR PRODUCTION ENQUIRIES

UNITED STATES AND CANADA
Info@SamuelFrench.com
1-866-598-8449

UNITED KINGDOM AND EUROPE
Plays@SamuelFrench-London.co.uk
020-7255-4302

Each title is subject to availability from Samuel French, depending upon country of performance. Please be aware that *SPAIN, SALTIMBANQUES,* and *GREEN MAN* may not be licensed by Samuel French in your territory. Professional and amateur producers should contact the nearest Samuel French office or licensing partner to verify availability.

FOREWORD
by Jim Knable

The Imaginary Plays are three plays I wrote at a particular time in my life and worked on at various others in sundry ways. They are not exactly a trilogy, but they might inform each other by being grouped together in publication. Think of them as an ever-shifting triptych. Two feature visual artists; another two invoke Spain or Spanish legends; two feature parents and children; two revolve (and one gallivants) around physical death; two are about failed romantic relationships. All are about people coming together after being apart. None end happily ever after, but they are not tragedies. All look towards what comes next. Each suggests that "imaginary" is distinct from "imagination" in that it implies the active effort to create something that was never there to help us deal with what gets taken away from us.

The order in which these plays were first drafted was *Saltimbanques/Spain/Green Man*, but *Saltimbanques* was significantly reworked after the first productions of *Spain* and *Spain* was significantly revised after *Green Man* was written and workshopped. The order they appear here makes the most sense to me in presenting them together, though each stands (and would likely be produced) on its own.

I am grateful for all the people and organizations that have been involved in developing these plays, many of whom I have endeavored to mention in the production notes before the plays. I am most grateful to my wife, Rosey, whom I met because she read and helped to produce another kind of imaginary play of mine and has been living in a world of imagination and reality with me ever since.

TABLE OF CONTENTS

Spain

SPAIN received its professional premiere at the Woolly Mammoth Theatre Company (Howard Shalwitz, Artistic Director; Kevin Moore, Managing Director) in Washington, D.C. on December 10, 2001. The production was directed by Tom Prewitt. The sets were by Robin Stapley, lights by Lisa Ogonowski, costumes by Rosemary Pardee, sound by Dave McKeever and props by Linda Evans. The dramaturg was Mary Resing. The stage manager was Margie Hasmall. The cast was as follows:

BARBARA . . . . .Emily Townley

CONQUISTADOR . . . . .Chris Lane

ANCIENT, ETC. . . . . Sarah Marshall

JOHN, ETC. . . . . .Andrew Wynn

DIVERSION . . . . Katie Barrett

SPAIN received its New York City premiere at The Summer Play Festival (Arielle Tepper, Producer and Founder) on July 18, 2006. The production was directed by Jeremy Dobrish and the stage manager was Alexis R. Prussack. The sets were by Dustin O'Neill, lights by Michael Gottlieb, costumes by Jessica Ford, and sound by Jill BC DuBoff. The cast was as follows:

BARBARA . . . . Stephanie Kurtzuba

CONQUISTADOR . . . . Michael Aronov

ANCIENT, ETC. . . . . Lisa Barnes

JOHN, ETC. . . . . David Rossmer

DIVERSION . . . . .Barb Pitts

SPAIN received its Off-Broadway premiere at MCC Theater (Bernard Telsey and Robert LuPone, Artistic Directors; William Cantler, Associate Artistic Director; Blake West, Executive Director) in New York City on October 10, 2007. The production was directed by Jeremy Dobrish and the stage manager was Alexis R. Prussack. The sets were by Beowulf Boritt, lights by Michael Gottlieb, costumes by Jenny Mannis, sound by Jill BC DuBoff, and props by Jeremy Lydic. The cast was as follows:

BARBARA . . . . .Annabella Sciorra

CONQUISTADOR . . . . Michael Aronov

ANCIENT, ETC. . . . . .Lisa Kron

JOHN, ETC. . . . . Erik Jensen

DIVERSION . . . . .Veanne Cox

CHARACTERS

BARBARA – A woman in her 30s.

CONQUISTADOR – A barbarous man in armor in his 30s or 40s.

ANCIENT – Also **OLD MAN, ROMAN, LAWYER, MONK, PSYCHIATRIST, GENERAL**. A woman in her 50s playing men's roles.

DIVERSION – A woman in her 30s. A little older than Barbara. No wiser.

JOHN – Barbara's husband. Also **GUITAR PLAYER, SHEPHERD** and **HORSE**.

TIME

The time is the present. Sort of.

Act One

(BARBARA and CONQUISTADOR are on opposite sides of the stage, unaware of each other.)

BARBARA. The heart of Spain is gold. Warm. Welcoming. Culture and cultures mixing, glowing in the high heat of the noon day sun.

CONQUISTADOR. The discovery of the New World marked a major turning point in my life. It opened up doors, gave me options I never knew I had. I found a genuine sense of purpose. I really felt like I was doing something for a change.

BARBARA. The soul of Spain.

CONQUISTADOR. Conquering. It is a great feeling. Meeting uncivilized people. Killing them, making them your slaves, what not.

BARBARA. Roosters.

CONQUISTADOR. For the first time in my life, I felt good about myself. My parents were proud of me. My wife wanted to sleep with me all the time.

BARBARA. Flamenco.

CONQUISTADOR. She told me I had become so much more virile. It was true.

BARBARA. The sweet sea smell of Barcelona.

CONQUISTADOR. My sexual appetite was insatiable. And I sated it quite often. Usually with my wife.

BARBARA. Red and Black and Yellow.

CONQUISTADOR. Ah, the New World, the new me.

BARBARA. Ferdinand and Isabella.

CONQUISTADOR. This helmet.

BARBARA. Picasso.

CONQUISTADOR. This beautiful shiny thing.

BARBARA. Gaudi.

CONQUISTADOR. Sometimes at night, I just sit on my bed and hold it on my lap.

BARBARA. Dali.

CONQUISTADOR. Trace the engraving. Look at my face in the reflection.

BARBARA. Lorca.

CONQUISTADOR. Who else gets to wear something like this?

BARBARA. Art.

CONQUISTADOR. The Spanish blood is strong in our veins.

BARBARA. Music.

CONQUISTADOR. We go places and name them.

BARBARA. Fire in the belly. Nothing else like it.

CONQUISTADOR. And in the heat of battle. On my horse. This God-like thing on my head. I swing my sword down. I feel so… good. Really and truly good. Blessed.

BARBARA. I have never been to Spain.

CONQUISTADOR. And afterwards. Wipe off the blood, get off my horse, stick my feet in the new earth, drink with my friends, maybe rape a prisoner.

BARBARA. I don't know Spanish.

CONQUISTADOR. This is what I was made for. I believe that. Look at me. This is who I am. I love myself.

BARBARA. The heart of Spain is gold.

(A **GUITAR PLAYER** *appears, playing a fast Spanish dance song.* **BARBARA** *dances in place, facing the audience.* **CONQUISTADOR** *does the same. They stop. The guitar stops.*)

I first hallucinated him shortly after my husband of five years left me for some slut with a boob job.

(*Lights reveal* **CONQUISTADOR** *sitting on a sofa with his feet up.*)

He was sitting on my sofa with his feet up. His funny metal boots on my coffee table. I was not attracted to him in the traditional sense.

I knew immediately he was not a real human being. He looked like one, smelled like one; when he talked I heard his voice like I'd hear anyone else's. But he was quite obviously a delusionary fragment of a repressed childhood primal picture book memory, nothing more.

I asked him: Who are you?

CONQUISTADOR. They call me El Tigre.

BARBARA. I asked him: Why are you here?

CONQUISTADOR. I do not know. It is a great mystery to me.

BARBARA. I asked him: What century are you from?

CONQUISTADOR. Sixteenth, year of our Lord, bless us and protect us, amen.

BARBARA. I did not ask him about his profession. Obviously he was a Conquistador. A real Spanish Conquistador. Luckily, he spoke English.
I did ask him to take his metal boots off my coffee table. And if I could take his sword and helmet.

CONQUISTADOR. *(taking his boots off the coffee table)*
I will hold on to them, thank you.

BARBARA. And then I said: Where exactly were you before this and how do you think you got from that place to my apartment?

CONQUISTADOR. It is a strange story.

BARBARA. I called in sick to work. *(to him)* I want to hear it.

(**GUITAR PLAYER** *strums.*)

CONQUISTADOR. Well…

(stands)

It was a raid like any other. Screaming, burning dwellings, what not. We rode through this… I suppose you could call it an alley or street… past the charred huts and dead Indians. And we came to an odd structure. A temple of sorts. We had seen it from a distance. A pyramid of sorts. Very tall, many steps. We all liked the look of it and decided not to destroy it. We would instead use it to throw a festival. It was perfect.

I got off my horse with the others and climbed all those steps. I could hear my men behind me. Clomp, clomp, clomp. The air grew cooler, the breeze blew lightly. I came to a portal. An entrance. Inside, a fire was glowing. I walked in. I saw an ancient sitting before the fire.

(**CONQUISTADOR** *walks left, into a new space. An implied fire is on the ground. An* **ANCIENT** *sits before it. Silence.* **ANCIENT** *and* **CONQUISTADOR** *look at each other.*)

ANCIENT. Buenas noches.

(**CONQUISTADOR** *draws his sword and prepares to strike. He stops, suddenly, to correct.*)

CONQUISTADOR. Buenos días.

ANCIENT. Buenas noches, Señor.

CONQUISTADOR. No. Buenos días. *(pointing outside)* Días.

ANCIENT. No, Señor Tigre. Buenas noches.

CONQUISTADOR. At which point there was a bright flash of light like lightening and I saw a vision.

A man on a skeleton donkey. A monkey's head on his neck. A crowd of men in white robes and hoods surrounding him.

And then I became the man with the monkey head and the white hoods fell. All their eyes glowed red. And lion claws reached out from white sleeves to touch me. And I closed my eyes and heard a voice.

ANCIENT. The Mayan calendar is indicative of the high level of civilization, intelligence and world comprehension found within the Mayan culture. Days, weeks and months are counted as are all numbers with dots and lines. And on this day of the four dots and two lines, there is predicted a shift in the very nature of time and continuity. That is to say, your raid of our culture was prophesied and you are now to become the vessel of higher perception due to the fact that I already know everything and the rest of the village is dead.

(Stage left goes black.)

CONQUISTADOR. And then another flash of light and I found myself sitting on your furniture. *(beat)* Where am I?

BARBARA. We call it the United States of America.

CONQUISTADOR. America?

BARBARA. Yes. Look. Did I hear you say burn and kill people?

CONQUISTADORS. Savages.

BARBARA. Your sword. Oh God.

CONQUISTADOR. Blood of the savages. I would have washed it if I knew I was coming.

BARBARA. Suddenly I feel ill.

CONQUISTADOR. Plague?

BARBARA. Conscience. What an awful hallucination.

CONQUISTADOR. You are having a vision now?

BARBARA. I like Spain. I love Spain.

CONQUISTADOR. Good, I won't have to kill you.

BARBARA. But you represent everything I hate about Spain and mankind in general.

CONQUISTADOR. I don't understand you.

BARBARA. You are symbolic of fear and repression and colonization and everything evil.

CONQUISTADOR. Evil?

BARBARA. But I love Spain. Jesus. Why couldn't you have been Lorca or Picasso. Well no, not Picasso.

CONQUISTADOR. I am not evil.

BARBARA. Cervantes.

CONQUISTADOR. I am all good.

BARBARA. Dali.

CONQUISTADOR. I love myself.

BARBARA. I don't want to deal with this right now.

CONQUISTADOR. I'm not even going to rape you.

BARBARA. And that's when I left.

(*Black on all but* **BARBARA** *and* **DIVERSION**, *her best friend.*)

DIVERSION. Barbara, I'm worried about you.

BARBARA. You're always worried about me.

DIVERSION. I'm always concerned. Now I am worried, this is worry.

BARBARA. You don't believe me?

DIVERSION. I do. I truly believe you are delusional.

BARBARA. But why him? Of all the delusions…

DIVERSION. Do you need to come live with me?

BARBARA. What?

DIVERSION. Being alone so suddenly. You're not used to being alone. And the circumstances.

BARBARA. I don't want to live with you.

(*Beat.*)

DIVERSION. Why not?

BARBARA. I have a place. I live in a place. I'm okay.

DIVERSION. You're having conversations with conquistadors!

BARBARA. I shouldn't have told you.

DIVERSION. Why not? I'm your best friend.

BARBARA. It's not like I'm doing harm to myself.

DIVERSION. You're missing work.

BARBARA. I hate work.

DIVERSION. No, you don't.

BARBARA. I do. I really do. I'm sick of Escrow folders and phone calls to buyers and Roman with his goatee and his roaming hands. I want to quit.

DIVERSION. Quit? Quit and do what?

BARBARA. Go to Spain.

DIVERSION. You're obsessive.

BARBARA. You should encourage me.

DIVERSION. You don't even know Spanish.

BARBARA. Maybe the Conquistador will teach me.

(*Silence.*)

DIVERSION. I have to get back to work. Do you want me to say anything to Roman?

BARBARA. No, no. I already told him I was sick in bed.

DIVERSION. That's not the only place you're sick.

BARBARA. Go back to work. I'll call you tonight.

(**DIVERSION** *disappears. Lights shift.* **CONQUISTADOR** *is sitting with his helmet in his lap on the sofa. He looks at his face in its reflection.* **BARBARA** *stands above him.*)

You're still here.

CONQUISTADOR. Yes.

BARBARA. What are you doing?

CONQUISTADOR. Spending time with my helmet. It makes me feel peaceful.

BARBARA. Your helmet?

CONQUISTADOR. Yes. Look. Come look.

(**BARBARA** *walks cautiously over to* **CONQUISTADOR** *and sits beside him on the sofa. They look at the helmet together.*)

BARBARA. What are these designs?

CONQUISTADOR. Beautiful, no?

BARBARA. Yes. But what are they?

CONQUISTADOR. Tigers.

(*He looks up at her and smiles.*)

BARBARA. El Tigre.

CONQUISTADOR. Sí.

(*Silence.*)

BARBARA. I know that if I touched you, I would actually feel you.

CONQUISTADOR. I do not understand.

BARBARA. I know it without even trying. And I know I don't want to try.

CONQUISTADOR. To try what?

BARBARA. To touch you.

(**CONQUISTADOR** *looks at her. He places his hand on her breast.*)

CONQUISTADOR. Like this?

BARBARA. *(pushing his hand away quickly)*
Don't. I don't want that.

CONQUISTADOR. I am beginning to.

(**BARBARA** *stands and moves away from him.*)

Do not be afraid. I would not dishonor you without your permission.

BARBARA. You're a killer and a rapist.

CONQUISTADOR. Only with Savages.

BARBARA. They're not savages, they're human beings and you wiped them out of existence.

CONQUISTADOR. Where is your husband?

(*Silence.* **CONQUISTADOR** *holds up a photo frame with a picture of* **BARBARA** *and a man in it.*)

This painting. I found it in your bedroom. Very true to life, especially for a miniature.

BARBARA. It's a photograph. I'm not going to explain what that is.

CONQUISTADOR. This is your husband, is it not?

(*Beat.*)

BARBARA. It was.

CONQUISTADOR. He's dead?

(*Beat.*)

BARBARA. Yes.

CONQUISTADOR. He was killed in battle?

(**BARBARA** *laughs.* **CONQUISTADOR** *looks at her.*)

BARBARA. John never fought a battle in his life.

CONQUISTADOR. He was lame?

BARBARA. Yes, he was very lame. Lame, boring, cowardly, lying, cheating.

CONQUISTADOR. How did he die? Did somebody kill him?

(**BARBARA** *looks at his sword.*)

BARBARA. I killed him.

CONQUISTADOR. You?

BARBARA. Sure. I found him with another woman and killed both of them.

(*Silence.*)

CONQUISTADOR. Hm. Good. Did you kill them in sleep?

BARBARA. No. I killed them in the heat of their passion.

CONQUISTADOR. Good. Good.

BARBARA. You approve?

CONQUISTADOR. I would do the same to my wife if I found her with another.

BARBARA. Would you rape her first?

CONQUISTADOR. (*repulsed*) No. No. She's my wife.

BARBARA. Give me that picture.

(**BARBARA** *holds out her hand.* **CONQUISTADOR** *hands it to her.*)

CONQUISTADOR. Why do you still keep it?

(**BARBARA** *looks at him. She smashes the frame against the table, takes out the photo and rips it to shreds. Silence.*)

You are not going to stomp and spit on it?

(*Beat.* **BARBARA** *does so.*)

How do you feel?

(**BARBARA** *looks at him.*)

BARBARA. Savage.

(*Blackout.*)

VOICE OF THE ANCIENT. The position of Ancient in a community is one to be acquired only through perseverance, bravery and self-mastery. It is a position of supreme wisdom beyond all comprehension. Most Ancients are destined to be Ancient from birth. All they have to do is live long enough.

And then there is the question of madness.

*(Lights up on the full stage. The **ANCIENT** stands omnisciently. The **GUITAR PLAYER** plays flamenco bursts. **BARBARA** has **CONQUISTADOR**'s sword. She is practicing sword thrusts, lunging in place while **CONQUISTADOR** stands behind her, steadying her arm, his other arm at her waist.)*

ANCIENT. Madness and wisdom are necessary brothers. Wisdom does not rise from sanity. Madness does not result from ignorance. Madness is more ancient than wisdom. I eat hay and howl at the sun every morning.

CONQUISTADOR. Good. It is in your nature.

BARBARA. It is?

CONQUISTADOR. I am sure you dealt a swift and cruel death to your husband.

*(**BARBARA** stops.)*

BARBARA. What am I doing?

CONQUISTADOR. Reliving the death blow. You thrust your sword into him, his blood spilled in rivers on the ground. His head went rolling down the stone steps.

BARBARA. I don't have stone steps.

CONQUISTADOR. You took your bloody revenge at the peak of his betrayal.

BARBARA. Betrayal. Yes, right, I did.

CONQUISTADOR. Did he see you come in?

BARBARA. No. No, not at first. She saw me. She screamed. The sword went through his back and came out his chest. His mouth fell open. This is horrible. Am I saying this?

CONQUISTADOR. Yes, yes, tell me more.

BARBARA. I never killed anyone.

CONQUISTADOR. It is a great feeling, is it not? The power.

BARBARA. Power. Yes. Having the power to… kill him. Kill him.

(She thrusts.)

CONQUISTADOR. Yes!

BARBARA. Stab him through the heart!

CONQUISTADOR. It is beautiful!

BARBARA. Destroy him!

CONQUISTADOR. You have so much Duende! You are so strong!

(She stops.)

BARBARA. I am? I have what?

CONQUISTADOR. Duende. I want to take my armor off with you.

BARBARA. I don't think that's a good idea.

CONQUISTADOR. You would like to remove it for me.

BARBARA. We'd better keep the armor on in this relationship.

CONQUISTADOR. I am holding you around the waist.

BARBARA. Yes.

CONQUISTADOR. Why are you letting me?

(BARBARA *pulls out a phone and speaks out to* DIVERSION.)

BARBARA. And I couldn't really answer. But there was no denying it. Since he came, I had destroyed my husband's picture, allowed him to put his cold hand on my breast and held his sword.

(DIVERSION *is lit, standing with a phone while the* ANCIENT *gives her a metaphysical shoulder massage.*)

DIVERSION. You touched him.

BARBARA. We've touched each other.

DIVERSION. You're not supposed to be able to touch delusions.

BARBARA. That's what I'm trying to tell you. This is turning into something else.

DIVERSION. Roman asked about you.

BARBARA. Are you hearing me?

DIVERSION. He asked if you were really sick or if you were planning to quit soon.

BARBARA. I don't care.

DIVERSION. I told him he would have to ask you himself tomorrow. When you come in.

BARBARA. Do you want to meet the Conquistador?

DIVERSION. I'll be right there.

(**BARBARA** *hangs up. Dark on* **DIVERSION**.)

CONQUISTADOR. You can communicate with spirits?

BARBARA. What?

CONQUISTADOR. You were not talking to me, but when you were talking I thought I heard a small voice near us.

BARBARA. I was using a telephone. It was invented by Alexander Graham Bell. It lets people talk to each other without them having to be in the same place.

CONQUISTADOR. Why would anyone want to do that?

BARBARA. I don't know.

CONQUISTADOR. I do not feel that you have told me exactly where I am.

BARBARA. This is the future. You're a few hundred years past where you were before this.

CONQUISTADOR. Are you part of my vision?

BARBARA. You are part of mine.

(*A doorbell rings.* **CONQUISTADOR** *jumps back and grabs his sword.*)

It's all right. That was my doorbell. It's Diversion.

CONQUISTADOR. I don't understand.

BARBARA. My best friend. Diversion.

CONQUISTADOR. What does that mean?

BARBARA. Don't worry about it. You're about to meet her.

(*BARBARA opens the door.*)

(**DIVERSION** *steps in and yells at seeing the* **CONQUISTADOR.**)

(*He yells back.*)

(*Stunned silence.*)

DIVERSION. My God.

BARBARA. I told you.

DIVERSION. I'm seeing your delusion.

BARBARA. Two people can't see the same delusion.

DIVERSION. Can I touch him?

BARBARA. Can she?

CONQUISTADOR. Please.

(**DIVERSION** *touches him.*)

DIVERSION. Oh! My God. Look at him. His metal is cold.

BARBARA. His hands are cold.

DIVERSION. What about his face?

BARBARA. I don't know.

(**DIVERSION** *reaches out and touches his face. She holds her hand there.*)

DIVERSION. Oh…

BARBARA. Cold?

DIVERSION. Warm. Hot. Burning.

(**DIVERSION** *pulls her hand back gently.*)

Where did you come from?

CONQUISTADOR. It is a strange story.

DIVERSION. I want to hear it.

(**CONQUISTADOR** *looks at* **BARBARA.**)

BARBARA. Go on. Tell it. I'll get us drinks. What would you like?

DIVERSION. Jim Beam on the rocks.

BARBARA. I'll be right back.

(**BARBARA** *exits. Guitar strums.*)

CONQUISTADOR. It was a day like any other. Roaming the green fields of my countryside. Alone on my stallion. Crossing short wooden bridges over brooks. I came to a grove of trees and bushes. Beneath one tree sat an old man. I swung off my horse and stood before him.

(**CONQUISTADOR** *walks; lights follow him. The* **ANCIENT** *sits on the ground, leaning up against an implied tree.*)

Buenos días.

ANCIENT. A las cinco de la tarde.

CONQUISTADOR. Que?

ANCIENT. El niño come naranjas.

CONQUISTADOR. And all at once there was burst of light and I saw a vision.

A woman dressed in a flowing white gown, her hair falling down on her shoulders. Floating above the earth. Her lips move as if to speak, but I hear nothing. A dew drop. A lily shaft open. The crowning of a boy eating oranges.

And then another burst of light and I was here. And the woman I knew in her white dress was dressed like a man.

(*Lights up on stage right.* **BARBARA** *stands nonplussed with two drinks.*)

BARBARA. That wasn't the story you told me.

DIVERSION. It was beautiful.

BARBARA. What happened to killing and raping everybody?

(**CONQUISTADOR** *just looks at* **BARBARA.**)

DIVERSION. Barbara. Don't offend him. He would never do that. He is a knight. A noble knight.

BARBARA. He's a Conquistador!

DIVERSION. You are his Dulcinea. You are his lady in white.

BARBARA. What happened while I was in the kitchen?

CONQUISTADOR. I told the story of my journey here, my lady.

BARBARA. My lady? Now I'm my lady?

DIVERSION. He is quite obviously in love with you.

BARBARA. What happened to you? You were against this whole thing being real at all.

DIVERSION. People can change.

BARBARA. Stop. Stop.

(*BARBARA* passes the drinks off to *DIVERSION* and walks up to **CONQUISTADOR**.)

What have you done to my friend?

CONQUISTADOR. I told her my story.

BARBARA. Why does she get a different story than I do?

CONQUISTADOR. She is a different woman.

BARBARA. So she gets the pretty story about countrysides and brooks and I get the pillaging and burning story.

She gets a woman in a white dress and I get you on a skeleton donkey with a monkey head? I'm the one in mourning for something! I'm the one who needs soothing!

CONQUISTADOR. Mourning?

BARBARA. I'm stranded. I'm alone. My husband left me for a slut with a boob job.

CONQUISTADOR. You killed your husband and his lover.

DIVERSION. Barbara?

BARBARA. I didn't kill them. I just told you I did to make myself feel good.

(*Silence.* **BARBARA** *and* **CONQUISTADOR** *look at each other.*)

CONQUISTADOR. Did it feel good?

BARBARA. Yes.

DIVERSION. What is he talking about, Barbara?

(*Beat.* **BARBARA** *turns to* **DIVERSION.**)

BARBARA. He's talking about murder. He's talking about lust. He's talking about wind that blows over the heads of the dead. He is a cruel, barbaric man with a bloody sword at his waist, a hundred angry souls at his heels and desire stronger than anything you've ever known in his heart.

DIVERSION. Am I dreaming?

BARBARA. You don't belong here.

DIVERSION. Does he?

BARBARA. Yes. But only as I want him.

DIVERSION. Barbara, am I losing my mind?

BARBARA. No. You're the sane one. Go home and pretend you dreamt this. Leave the drinks for us. Go.

(**DIVERSION** *exits.* **BARBARA** *looks at* **CONQUISTADOR.**)

What are you, really?

CONQUISTADOR. What do you believe?

BARBARA. I don't know what to think.

CONQUISTADOR. Do not think.

BARBARA. Who do you think I am?

CONQUISTADOR. I am not thinking.

BARBARA. A woman in man's clothing? A vision?

CONQUISTADOR. Yes.

BARBARA. Which story is true?

CONQUISTADOR. Both.

(*A brilliant flash of white light. The* **ANCIENT** *stands and sings with the* **GUITAR PLAYER.** *The* **GUITAR PLAYER** *in Spanish, the* **ANCIENT** *in English.*)

(*As they sing* **BARBARA** *begins removing* **CONQUISTADOR** *'s armor with his help and silent instruction. This is not erotic. It is simple.*)

GUITAR PLAYER.	ANCIENT.
En mita del mar	Out in the sea
había una piedra	was a stone.
y se sentaba mi compaerita	My girl sat down
a contarle sus penas	to tell it her pains.
Tan solamente a la Tierra	Only to the Earth
le cuento lo que me pasa,	do I tell my troubles,
porque en el mundo no encuentro	for nowhere in the world
persona e mi confianza	do I find anyone I trust.

(**CONQUISTADOR** *stands in his Sixteenth Century underwear.* **BARBARA** *motions for him to sit on the floor by the table. She pulls a bottle of whiskey out from under the table, drinks from it. He drinks. She drinks. He drinks.*)

(*She reaches under the table and pulls out a large travel book. She opens it and shows it to* **CONQUISTADOR.**)

BARBARA. It's been my fantasy for a long time.

CONQUISTADOR. Spain.

BARBARA. I wanted to go there with John. I wanted that to be the place where we found love again. I wanted a country to love.

CONQUISTADOR. You want love.

BARBARA. Wanted.

CONQUISTADOR. And now?

BARBARA. Tell me what it feels like to kill someone.

CONQUISTADOR. You already know.

BARBARA. A whole civilization. What is that like?

CONQUISTADOR. It is like nothing else.

BARBARA. It makes you feel strong.

CONQUISTADOR. Yes.

BARBARA. Because they can't defend themselves against your weapons.

CONQUISTADOR. Yes.

BARBARA. And you can do anything you want with them?

CONQUISTADOR. Yes.

>   *(BARBARA drinks.)*

BARBARA. Cut off their heads.

CONQUISTADOR. Of course.

BARBARA. Disembowel them.

CONQUISTADOR. Certainly.

BARBARA. Cut off their balls.

CONQUISTADOR. Occasionally.

BARBARA. You ride into town with your men, in your armor; you all stink like horses…

CONQUISTADOR. Horses, oh yes!

BARBARA. The villagers stare up at you terrified, helpless, you don't even see them as human…

CONQUISTADOR. Villagers?

BARBARA. The weak, the peasants…

CONQUISTADOR. Peasants, pthuh…

BARBARA. Then what?

CONQUISTADOR. Kill the peasants!

BARBARA. Yes! You hit your heels on your horse and ride through them, swooping your sword, hacking, slashing…

CONQUISTADOR. *(suggesting)* Chopping?

BARBARA. Chopping up and down!
You take up a fiery lance, you hurl it through the air, it soars, fire trailing, down into the hut where the men hold ceremonies; it bursts into flames.

CONQUISTADOR. Many, many flames!

BARBARA. You burn it all down, you leave nothing standing. The dirt roads run muddy with blood.

CONQUISTADOR. Muddy blood.

BARBARA. You drink the blood, your mouth is red, you run, screaming battle cries, killing everything in your path, even your own men, your lust consumes you.

CONQUISTADOR. You are very good at this.

BARBARA. You burn with death and pain, painless pain because you feel nothing but overpowering joy, you spin your arms and wave your sword and stand on top off all the bodies, like a mountain, you stand on top and breathe in the smell of torn-out flesh!

*(**CONQUISTADOR** drinks.)*

CONQUISTADOR. Yes, all that. I do that.

This drink is good. What is it?

BARBARA. Whiskey.

John drank it, his bottle.

BARBARA.	**CONQUISTADOR.**
(gleefully, with him)	*(as before with the portrait)*
Why do I still keep it?	Why do you still keep it?

(She takes another swig and hurls it offstage.)

(Crash!)

(They laugh.)

I could destroy everything.

The couch. We bought it together.

*(She goes to the couch and tears into the pillows, hurling them, violent and crazy. **CONQUISTADOR** helps some, but is no match for her fury.)*

What else? More pictures? I have more pictures. Dishes? The sheets? His smell still on them. Everything here we had together, I could destroy everything!

CONQUISTADOR. You are amazing.

BARBARA. I could destroy, myself, I could destroy... I could...

(She flops down on the remains of the couch.)

Too much, too fast. Spinning.

CONQUISTADOR. Spinning. Yes, spinning your arms.

BARBARA. Room spinning.

Can't look.

Too much…

(She collapses.)

CONQUISTADOR. Barbara?

(Lights rise on the **ANCIENT***, fall on* **CONQUISTADOR** *and* **BARBARA***.)*

(While the **ANCIENT** *talks, he changes into a very corporate looking business suit.)*

ANCIENT. There is always the question of violence.

Violence can come from outside or inside.

(pause)

Occasionally, it is necessary to make a sacrifice.

The Ancient will choose who to sacrifice.

Take him to the temple. Tie him to the rock.

Hold the point of the blade over his heart and then… push it in.

There is usually screaming and spattering of blood.

This is to be expected. No one likes to be sacrificed.

But then the sky opens up along a bright white crack. The moon is invented. The dark grass of hills holding trees waves in sea green, the whole of souls goes spinning; and names are remembered. Empires fall. Countries lose their borders. Anything is then possible.

All are capable of such violence.

(Light falls on **ANCIENT***. Rises on* **CONQUISTADOR** *and* **BARBARA***. Morning. They are sleeping, passed out on the floor.)*

(A key in a lock is heard.)

(A door swings open.)

*(***JOHN** *[the* **GUITAR PLAYER***] walks on carrying a guitar in a case and a trunk full of his clothes. He looks spent and dejected. At first he does not see* **BARBARA** *and*

CONQUISTADOR. *He lays down his load and flops onto the couch. Now he notices the bodies. He peers at them inquisitively. He notices the armor lying near the table.)*

JOHN. Barbara? Barbara?

BARBARA. *(in sleep)* John?

JOHN. Barbara, I'm back. I'm sorry I left you. What is this man doing on the floor and why is there armor in our house?

BARBARA. John?

(She wakes.)

John?!

(sitting bolt upright)

John?!!

JOHN. You wouldn't believe what I've been through. And now this. Christ, what a strange world.

BARBARA. What are you doing here?

JOHN. Yolanda dumped me for some guy with big muscles and no neck. I realized I made a mistake leaving you. I came back. I hope you can forgive me. Do you want to tell me who this guy is?

BARBARA. You're gone.

JOHN. I'm right here.

BARBARA. I killed you.

JOHN. Honey, I think you're still a little bit asleep.

BARBARA. I walked in on you and the slut with the boob job having sex in our bed and I slaughtered you both.

JOHN. Barbara, I'm right here. I'm alive. Yolanda's alive. I wish she was dead, but she's alive. You're in the middle of a dream or something.

BARBARA. Spain.

JOHN. What?

BARBARA. Spain.

(BARBARA stands.)

JOHN. You want to talk about Spain right now? Why don't you go splash some water on your face. Would you like me to make coffee?

(**BARBARA** *walks over to the armor and picks up the sword.*)

What are you doing? Jesus, what the hell is that?

BARBARA. Spain.

(**BARBARA** *puts the point of the sword against* **JOHN**'s *chest.*)

JOHN. Honey, what are you going to do here? Kill me?

BARBARA. Sure.

(**BARBARA** *drives the sword into* **JOHN**. *Lights go white. A phone rings. Black.*)

Hello?

(*Lights back on.* **DIVERSION** *stands next to* **ROMAN** *[*ANCIENT*] stage left.* **DIVERSION** *holds the phone.* **BARBARA** *stands calmly with the sword at her side, her dead bleeding husband on the sofa and the* **CONQUISTADOR** *passed out on the floor.*)

DIVERSION. Barbara, it's me. I'm standing here with Roman. We're both worried about you.

BARBARA. Concerned?

DIVERSION. Worried. I had the strangest dream about you last night. I was telling Roman about it. Why aren't you coming into work?

ROMAN. Let me talk to her.

DIVERSION. Roman wants to talk to you.

ROMAN. Barbara, look, I'm not angry with you for lying about being sick. You're obviously going through some period of mental instability resulting from being rejected by your husband. I understand. I've read lots of books where that happens. But we need you here, Barbara. We need you in Escrow, we need you on the phone, we need your magic touch. I think it might even help you with your feelings of worthlessness to come in and make yourself busy. I've heard that it's good for people in your state to keep going to work and, in fact, work even harder than usual to make up for the emptiness in their lives. And look, Barbara, I don't want to have to threaten you, but if you don't come in by tomorrow, I'll fire you. So why don't you come in today. What do you say?

BARBARA. I quit.

ROMAN. Barbara, don't do this.

BARBARA. If I came into that office, I would hack all of you to pieces with a long and blood-stained Spanish sword.

ROMAN. Maybe you should think about this for a little while. I'll call back tomorrow.

BARBARA. If you call me, I'll track you down and murder your whole family.

ROMAN. Jesus, Barbara, you've really gone off the deep end, haven't you.

BARBARA. Yes.

ROMAN. Well. We'll miss you.

BARBARA. Thanks. Put Diversion on, would you?

ROMAN. No problem. *(handing* **DIVERSION** *the phone)* For you.

    *(***ROMAN** *walks off.)*

DIVERSION. What's going on here, Barb?

BARBARA. I'm going through some very important changes.

DIVERSION. Yeah? That sounds positive.

BARBARA. I just quit my job.

DIVERSION. Barbara!

BARBARA. It was easy. It felt good. Just like when I drove this sword into my husband's chest. That's the thing I've realized, you know? It's so easy to simply do these things.

DIVERSION. What are you talking about?

BARBARA. Do you remember your dream from last night? The one with me and the Conquistador? Where he told you what you wanted to hear and I told you the way it was. That really happened. Things like that really happen. Do you understand? No, you probably don't. Why don't you just pretend I'm crazy.

DIVERSION. I think you need help, Barbara.

BARBARA. Good, good.

DIVERSION. I know you have a thing against shrinks, but this guy I've been seeing lately...

BARBARA. I don't care about your personal life. Go give Roman a blow job or something.

DIVERSION. Barbara!

BARBARA. You can use my desk if you like.

DIVERSION. I can't believe...

BARBARA. No, you can't. Good bye.

(BARBARA *hangs up. Dark on* DIVERSION. CONQUISTADOR *is sitting up at this point, watching* BARBARA. *She nods over to* JOHN. CONQUISTADOR *looks at him inquisitively.*)

CONQUISTADOR. Dead.

BARBARA. Dead.

CONQUISTADOR. Who is he?

BARBARA. Husband.

CONQUISTADOR. Again?

BARBARA. Yeah.

CONQUISTADOR. You killed his ghost.

BARBARA. Sure.

CONQUISTADOR. My head hurts.

BARBARA. You have a hang-over.

CONQUISTADOR. Barbara?

BARBARA. *(jarred at hearing him say her name)* Yeah?

CONQUISTADOR. Why am I still here?

(*Beat.*)

BARBARA. Beats me. But do me a favor. Don't talk like a real human being.

(**BARBARA** *starts to walk off.*)

CONQUISTADOR. Where are you going?

BARBARA. Wash the blood off.

(**BARBARA** *exits.* **CONQUISTADOR** *looks at* **JOHN**. **JOHN** *opens his eyes and talks nonchalantly to* **CONQUISTADOR**.)

JOHN. I met Yolanda in a snow storm. I was walking home from the Metro. She was all bundled up like an Eskimo, getting her mail I guess. Very cute. I said something stupid like: Nice snow storm, huh? She laughed. Her breath was hot. It puffed. Then she said: Do you want to come inside? And I thought she was kidding. She couldn't even see my face and I couldn't see hers. But then she took my hand and led me in. All we knew were each other's voices, but she just brought me into her house. And I started to take off my coat but she stopped me, wouldn't even let me take down the hood.

Not yet, she said, and she reached down to her pants and unbuttoned them. And I did the same with mine. And then both of us were standing with no pants or underwear in our big coats and hoods, all bundled up on top. And she pulled me against a wall and we did it like that. The coats, you know, they were squeaking against each other. I put the hole in my hood next to the hole in hers and we breathed on each other. It was like hiding under a blanket. It was wonderful.

When it was over, she said: I will if you will. And we both took off our coats and hoods and laughed and laughed and laughed. Not because we knew each other. Because we didn't.

But then we tried to.

And I left my wife with all her books about Spain and all her misery and boredom.

JOHN. *(cont.)*

But then something went wrong.

Something always goes wrong.

And here I am.

Who are you?

CONQUISTADOR. They call me El Tigre. Do you know that you're dead?

(Beat. JOHN *looks down at his body and the blood on his shirt.)*

JOHN. How did that happen?

CONQUISTADOR. Your wife stabbed you.

JOHN. Christ. When?

CONQUISTADOR. Before I woke up.

JOHN. I'm dead?

CONQUISTADOR. Yes.

JOHN. I don't feel dead.

CONQUISTADOR. If she finds you alive, she'll kill you again.

JOHN. Where is she?

CONQUISTADOR. Washing your blood off her hands.

(Beat. JOHN *jumps up.)*

JOHN. I tried, right?

*(*CONQUISTADOR *shrugs.)*

Good luck.

*(*JOHN *runs to his suitcase and guitar, grabs them and leaves.)*

*(*BARBARA *enters, refreshed.* CONQUISTADOR *looks at her.* BARBARA *looks at the empty couch.)*

BARBARA. Where is he?

CONQUISTADOR. He left.

BARBARA. He was dead!

CONQUISTADOR. I told him.

BARBARA. What did he say?

CONQUISTADOR. He told me the story of how he met his lover.

(*Beat.*)

BARBARA. Did he leave through the front door or did angels come and get him or something?

CONQUISTADOR. Front door.

(**BARBARA** *grabs the sword and charges out the front door.* **CONQUISTADOR** *sits on the sofa.* **ANCIENT** *enters and sits next to* **CONQUISTADOR**. **CONQUISTADOR** *notices, but is not surprised.*)

What am I doing here?

ANCIENT. Being useful.

CONQUISTADOR. When can I leave?

ANCIENT. When you're done.

CONQUISTADOR. Done what?

ANCIENT. Participating in a ritualistic experiment.

CONQUISTADOR. Who are you?

ANCIENT. Ancient.

CONQUISTADOR. Besides that.

ANCIENT. Old man.

CONQUISTADOR. Why do I have two different memories of how I got here?

ANCIENT. They're the same.

CONQUISTADOR. Why won't Barbara sleep with me?

ANCIENT. Because you told her you're a rapist.

(**BARBARA** *enters, sword in hand, out of breath. She sees the* **ANCIENT**.)

BARBARA. Now what.

CONQUISTADOR. Did you find him?

BARBARA. No. I frightened the neighbors. I think someone is going to call the police.

ANCIENT. You must be Barbara.

BARBARA. Yeah. What are you?

CONQUISTADOR. He's the one who sent me here.

BARBARA. Oh.

You're all-knowing?

ANCIENT. Usually.

BARBARA. How about a little enlightenment?

ANCIENT. You are acting out a Freudian fantasy based on a Jungian nightmare, served to you by an Andalusian Mayan Soul Prophet by way of a delusionary fragment of a repressed childhood primal collective unconscious memory.

BARBARA. You talk like a textbook.

ANCIENT. I have to be going now.

BARBARA/CONQUISTADOR. Wait!

ANCIENT. You'll see me again.

BARBARA. What are we supposed to do?

ANCIENT. Whatever you want.

BARBARA. Is my husband dead or alive?

*(**ANCIENT** shrugs.)*

Is any of this really happening?

*(**ANCIENT** nods.)*

Why him?

*(Silence. **CONQUISTADOR** looks at her, a little hurt. **ANCIENT** shakes his head.)*

Am I a murderer?

ANCIENT. No.

BARBARA. Is he?

ANCIENT. Good bye.

*(**ANCIENT** walks off.)*

BARBARA/CONQUISTADOR. Wait!

*(Silence. **BARBARA** and **CONQUISTADOR** look at each other.)*

Put your armor back on.

*(Lights move to **DIVERSION**, who is speaking with her implied **PSYCHIATRIST**.)*

DIVERSION. He was dressed in shiny silver metal. It curved around his chest, rose at his shoulders, fell in patterns down his back. His beard was rough and brown. His face was warm, I touched it with my palm. It was so incredibly lifelike. And Barbara was there, too. She was acting crazy, like a wild animal. She tried to make him seem less good. She tried to make him take back the story about the green country and the old man. She doesn't make any sense.

I tried to suggest she come in and talk to you.

(PSYCHIATRIST [ANCIENT] appears.)

PSYCHIATRIST. Good. That was the right thing to do. Tell me more about the man in shiny silver. Were you attracted to him?

DIVERSION. Not in the traditional sense.
There was something familiar about him.

PSYCHIATRIST. You mentioned a story.

DIVERSION. Yes. It was beautiful. He was Don Quixote. But Barbara said he was a Conquistador.

PSYCHIATRIST. How do you feel about Barbara?

DIVERSION. She's lost her marbles.

PSYCHIATRIST. Are you attracted to Barbara?

DIVERSION. I don't want to think about that.

(Lights go stage right. **CONQUISTADOR** *is back in his armor.)*

BARBARA. We need to make a pact.

CONQUISTADOR. A pact?

BARBARA. A pact between you and me that says we are allies.

CONQUISTADOR. I do not–

BARBARA. Sure you do. Allies. In war. Whatever happens. You protect me, I protect you.

CONQUISTADOR. How will you protect me?

BARBARA. You've seen me in action.

CONQUISTADOR. Yes.

BARBARA. We're in whatever this is together. And I think it's a fight. I think we're fighting something. That's why you're here.

CONQUISTADOR. What are we fighting?

BARBARA. We don't know. Right? But we're here. Look. Give me your sword.

CONQUISTADOR. What are you going to do with it?

BARBARA. Trust me.

(CONQUISTADOR *hands her his sword.*)

Get on your knees.

(CONQUISTADOR *does so.*)

(BARBARA *passes the sword from one of his shoulders to the other.*)

I knight you in the name of the fight whatever it is. Rise.

(*He does. She hands him the sword.*)

Now do it to me.

CONQUISTADOR. I–

(BARBARA *gets on her knees.*)

BARBARA. Do it.

CONQUISTADOR. I have never met a woman like you.

BARBARA. Sure you have. Knight me.

(*Beat.* CONQUISTADOR *knights her.*)

CONQUISTADOR. I knight you, Barbara– what is your full name?

BARBARA. Tusenbach.

CONQUISTADOR. I knight you Barbara Tusenbach in the name of Spain, Her Majesty, God–

BARBARA. The fight.

CONQUISTADOR. The fight. And in the name of Duende.

BARBARA. Duende? What's that?

CONQUISTADOR. Rise.

(BARBARA *rises.*)

BARBARA. What's Duende?

(The sound of sirens.)

CONQUISTADOR. What is that noise?

BARBARA. Sirens. They're coming.

CONQUISTADOR. Who?

BARBARA. Our adversaries. What is Duende?

CONQUISTADOR. Everything you cannot name, but already said.

(The sirens get louder.)

BARBARA. Is this what it feels like before a battle?

CONQUISTADOR. Barbara.

BARBARA. Is this the feeling you get? Is this the Duende?

CONQUISTADOR. Barbara Tusenbach.

BARBARA. Yes, El Tigre.

CONQUISTADOR. I have never been in a battle.

BARBARA. What?

CONQUISTADOR. I have never been out of Spain.

BARBARA. What?

CONQUISTADOR. I have never killed anyone.

BARBARA. What are you talking about?

CONQUISTADOR. I wander around the green countryside pretending. I pretend. I am not even married.

BARBARA. What the hell are you talking about?!

CONQUISTADOR. I'm pretending this right now.

BARBARA. Bullshit. Bullshit. This is the truest thing I've ever felt.

CONQUISTADOR. I'm pretending. You're not.

BARBARA. What does that mean?

CONQUISTADOR. I am not a conquistador.

(A screeching of tires up to a house. A beating on the front door.)

COP VOICE. Mrs. Tusenbach! Mrs. Tusenbach, this is the police! We have you surrounded. Open up, or we'll break down your door!

(**BARBARA** *looks at* **CONQUISTADOR**. *She takes his helmet off his head and puts in on hers. She takes his sword.*)

COP VOICE. Mrs. Tusenbach, we know what you've done! Let us in!

(**BARBARA** *charges for the door with a terrible battle yell.*)

Act Two

*(An interrogation room. **BARBARA** sits across from **LAWYER** [ANCIENT]. She is dressed in an orange numbered jumpsuit.)*

LAWYER. Mrs. Tusenbach. Let's talk about the carving knife.

BARBARA. What carving knife?

LAWYER. The one you used to attack the policemen at your door and stab your husband.

BARBARA. The Spanish sword?

LAWYER. No. The carving knife. What were you thinking when you picked it up?

BARBARA. The sword?

LAWYER. Sure, the carving knife.

BARBARA. I wasn't thinking.

LAWYER. Were you defending yourself?

BARBARA. I was attacking.

LAWYER. You were attacking your husband and the police.

BARBARA. I was fighting with Duende.

LAWYER. Is Duende the name of the Conquistador?

BARBARA. He's not really a Conquistador.

LAWYER. Let's talk about him.

BARBARA. Who the hell are you, anyway?

LAWYER. I'm your attorney. I introduced myself when I came in. Do you remember that?

BARBARA. Who can believe what anyone says when they introduce themselves?

LAWYER. Mrs. Tusenbach, is there a history of mental instability in your family?

BARBARA. No, my family is the only family in the world that acts completely rationally.

LAWYER. You should try to answer my questions cooperatively, Mrs. Tusenbach. I'm the one who might save you from a very long prison sentence.

(Beat.)

BARBARA. I met him shortly after my husband of five years left me for some slut with a boob job. He was sitting on my sofa with his feet up. His funny metal boots on my coffee table. I was not attracted to him in the traditional sense.

LAWYER. You spoke to him.

BARBARA. It was easy.

LAWYER. Did you think there was anything odd about the situation?

BARBARA. I told him to take his metal boots off my coffee table.

LAWYER. Other than that.

BARBARA. His sword was bloody.

LAWYER. The sword you used to stab your husband and the–

BARBARA. Yes. It was bloody.

(to herself)

How could it be bloody if he wasn't a conquistador? I saw blood.

LAWYER. Whose blood?

BARBARA. Mayan blood. Blood of the people he had slaughtered.

LAWYER. Uh-huh. Go on.

BARBARA. How could I have seen blood if what he said wasn't true?

(Lights switch to down right.)

*(**DIVERSION** stands there holding an orange.)*

DIVERSION. Barbara always was a little, you know, out there. But she controlled it. She worked hard at the office. She was very good at talking to people on the phone and dealing with Escrow. But on her lunch breaks, you know, we would talk, I was her best friend– I am her best friend, and she would say things every once in while. "I'm feeling restless." "John doesn't pay attention to me." She had this fantasy about Spain. It started two years ago. She saw a movie or something. She started buying books. Maps. She toyed with taking a Spanish class, but she didn't have time and John was very unsupportive of the whole thing.

I don't blame her for stabbing him. He was a real bastard. She shouldn't be punished too harshly for that. I was more disturbed by the other stabbing. That poor man. He was just doing his job.

(She bites into the orange skin and lets the juice run down her chin.)

(Lights flip over to the table.)

BARBARA. Is that a one-way mirror?

LAWYER. Depends on which side you're on.

*(**BARBARA** stands and walks over to the implied mirror, behind the **LAWYER**. Lights illuminate what she sees in it– the **CONQUISTADOR**.)*

What are you going to do? Make faces at them?

*(**BARBARA** ignores **LAWYER**. She studies the **CONQUISTADOR**. He is dressed like an Andalusian peasant. He mirrors her in a variety of gestures. Finally, their hands meet where the plane of the mirror would be. They lock fingers. The **LAWYER** watches, fascinated.)*

Barbara?

*(**CONQUISTADOR** pulls **BARBARA** out of the scene. Only they are lit.)*

BARBARA. Where are we?

CONQUISTADOR. Green fields. Windmills. Wild horses and deep bark trees far off.

(**BARBARA** *takes a moment to look around.*)

BARBARA. It's beautiful.

(beat)

How did you get out of my living room?

CONQUISTADOR. White light.

(**BARBARA** *studies* **CONQUISTADOR.**)

Are you angry with me?

BARBARA. *(laughs)* Jesus, you aren't a Conquistador at all.

CONQUISTADOR. No.

BARBARA. Where did you get all the fancy armor?

CONQUISTADOR. I do not know. I only know I was in it when I met you. And I had things in my head that explained it.

BARBARA. Stories?

CONQUISTADOR. Yes.

BARBARA. You see this outfit I have on? I'm in prison. What do you make of that? You show up and tell me you're a killer and I get all inspired and stab my husband with a carving knife.

CONQUISTADOR. You stabbed him with my sword.

BARBARA. That's not what they say.

CONQUISTADOR. Who?

BARBARA. The Inquisition! What does it matter what anyone calls themselves.

CONQUISTADOR. You are angry.

BARBARA. Yes. No. I was. Now I'm just jaded and world-weary.

CONQUISTADOR. A shepherd.

BARBARA. What?

CONQUISTADOR. A shepherd.

(*An Andalusian* **SHEPHERD** *[***GUITAR PLAYER***] is lit. He carries a staff and a guitar slung over his shoulder, on his back.*)

(**BARBARA** *and* **CONQUISTADOR** *look at him.*)

BARBARA. Jesus.

(**SHEPHERD** *points to his mouth and shakes his head.*)

CONQUISTADOR. He is mute.

BARBARA. He looks like John.

CONQUISTADOR. *(to* **SHEPHERD***)* She is not from around here.

BARBARA. What is this place?

CONQUISTADOR. Andalusia.

BARBARA. What is this place to you?

CONQUISTADOR. My home.

BARBARA. Spain.

CONQUISTADOR. Yes.

BARBARA. This is Spain?

CONQUISTADOR. Welcome.

(**SHEPHERD** *hands off his staff to* **CONQUISTADOR** *and swings his guitar into playing position. He sings.*)

SHEPHERD.
SI MI CORAZÓN TUVIERA
BIERIERITAS E CRISTAR,
TE ASOMARAS Y LO VIERAS
GOTAS DE SANGRE LLORAR.

(*Silence.* **SHEPHERD** *swings his guitar back over his shoulder and takes his staff back from* **CONQUISTADOR***. He walks off.*)

BARBARA. I thought he was mute.

CONQUISTADOR. He is.

BARBARA. He has a very nice singing voice for a mute.

CONQUISTADOR. He sings the deep song.

BARBARA. It was charming.

CONQUISTADOR. Siguiriya.

BARBARA. I don't know Spanish.

CONQUISTADOR. "If my heart had windowpanes of glass, you'd look inside and see it crying drops of blood."

BARBARA. I'm feeling angry.

CONQUISTADOR. Why?

BARBARA. What the hell is going on here?

CONQUISTADOR. You are where you always wanted to be.

BARBARA. Stop. Why did I see blood on your sword if you didn't kill anyone?

CONQUISTADOR. It was not truly my sword.

BARBARA. What is your real name?

CONQUISTADOR. Pepe.

BARBARA. *(disgusted)* God.

CONQUISTADOR. The discovery of the New World marked a major turning point in my life.

BARBARA. Excuse me?

CONQUISTADOR. Conquering. It is a great feeling.

BARBARA. Stop.

CONQUISTADOR. We go places and name them.

BARBARA. Stop. Why are you saying those things?

CONQUISTADOR. I said them before.

BARBARA. You're not a conquistador anymore.

CONQUISTADOR. The heart of Spain is gold.

BARBARA. Who the fuck are you?

CONQUISTADOR. It is a wind that blows over the heads of the dead.

BARBARA. What?

CONQUISTADOR. Duende.

BARBARA. What the fuck is Duende?

CONQUISTADOR. Dónde está el duende?

> *(A* **MONK [ANCIENT]** *enters, dressed in a white robe and black scapular. New lighting, suggesting a church. The* **MONK** *gets into prayer position downstage.* **BARBARA** *and* **CONQUISTADOR** *watch him.)*

BARBARA. What happened?

CONQUISTADOR. Shhh. He is praying.

MONK.

Dominus padre om.

Et spiritus sancti uno.

Duende, Duende, Duende.

Barbara, Barbara, Barbara.

BARBARA. What is this?

(*Silence.* **MONK** *turns and looks at* **BARBARA.** *Silence. He stands. He walks to her and places his hand over her heart. She is frozen.*)

MONK.

¿Dónde está el duende?

What do you want?

(*Silence.* **BARBARA** *is in a trance.*)

BARBARA. I want faces made of glass. No more soft lips or cheeks or baby smiles. I want sharp angles and grey lines. I want eyes like lifeless diamonds. I want to live touching nothing. I want to float invisible.

(**MONK** *holds out his arms, Christlike.* **CONQUISTADOR** *walks to him and disrobes him. Underneath his robe,* **MONK** *is* **LAWYER.** *Lights shift back to the way they were at the top of the act. Back in the little room with* **BARBARA** *and* **LAWYER.** **CONQUISTADOR** *and the* **MONK**'*s robe are gone.*)

LAWYER. Barbara?

(**BARBARA** *stares at* **LAWYER.**)

Are you all right?

(**BARBARA** *laughs.*)

BARBARA. Now who are you?

LAWYER. I'm your lawyer. I think you just had some sort of episode.

BARBARA. Several, actually.

LAWYER. You said some things.

BARBARA. I bet I did.

LAWYER. You said: faces made of glass. What does that mean?

BARBARA. If my heart had windowpanes of glass.

LAWYER. Barbara, I think the next step is to bring in a psychiatrist.

BARBARA. Will that be you, too?

LAWYER. I don't think we're going to have much trouble with the insanity plea.

BARBARA. What are all these pieces?

LAWYER. Pieces?

BARBARA. Monks and Mayans and Conquistadors.

LAWYER. Yes, I completely agree. I think perhaps our meeting is done for now.

BARBARA. What's next? You know? ¿Donde esta el duende?

LAWYER. Absolutely. Nothing to worry about.

(*MATADOR (JOHN) enters with a flourish.* **BARBARA** *collapses laughing.*)

Yes. Keep laughing. That's wonderful. This is all on tape. Nothing to worry about at all.

(*The* **MATADOR** *looks to be sizing up* **BARBARA** *as if she were a bull. She starts to play the role, making her fingers into horns and brushing the ground with her foot.* **LAWYER** *watches.*)

Beautiful. That's… amazing. Keep going, don't stop.

(**BARBARA** *charges* **MATADOR** *and gores him.*)

(*Lights shift to illuminate* **DIVERSION**, *dressed as a Flamenco Dancer. She dances in silence for a few moments. Then speaks and dances at the same time.*)

DIVERSION. The funny thing is: I know Spanish. I've read Lorca backwards and forwards. I took Flamenco classes at the gym. But that was a phase, you know? I got over it and settled down. Now I have a steady job and pets and all the comfortable amenities of American life. So I suppose, really, I was as discouraging as John when it came to Barbara's obsession. I wanted her to get over it. It only reminded me of a way I used to be. Young. How depressing. Younger. Than now. Now I see a shrink and pay my bills on time.

(Lights shift.)

(CONQUISTADOR *leads* **BARBARA** *along a narrow cliff ledge.)*

CONQUISTADOR. Careful. It is a great distance down from this cliff.

BARBARA. Where are we going?

CONQUISTADOR. To the valley. Over that stream. Through those woods.

BARBARA. What is our destination?

CONQUISTADOR. My home.

BARBARA. Your house.

CONQUISTADOR. We must get there before dark.

BARBARA. What happens after dark?

CONQUISTADOR. Wolves.

BARBARA. It's strange. You're nothing like you were, but it's still you.

CONQUISTADOR. We will also have to pass through a waterfall. Up ahead, beyond that ridge.

BARBARA. Do I seem different?

CONQUISTADOR. It is always hard to understand you.

BARBARA. Other than that.

CONQUISTADOR. Yes. You keep changing.

BARBARA. Are you sad that you aren't a Conquistador anymore?

CONQUISTADOR. A little. I am glad we could meet again.

BARBARA. Oh? Why is that?

CONQUISTADOR. You help me to understand myself.

BARBARA. Oh.

CONQUISTADOR. Come. We are nearly to the waterfall.

(They exit.)

(*Light to* **DIVERSION**, *no longer dancing, just fanning herself.*)

DIVERSION. I used to watch her at her desk. She'd stare off into space, stare like she saw something there. And then she'd come to me with her latest map or picture, some story she found, some word. I would pretend I didn't know what the words were, pretend the fantasies she had didn't used to be my own. You reach a point where fantasizing like that is just embarrassing. When it's time to look at where you really are.

(*She looks down at her fan. She walks off.*)

(**CONQUISTADOR** *and* **BARBARA** *enter. This is now* **CONQUISTADOR**'s *home. A mat for sleeping, not much else.*)

BARBARA. This is where you live?

CONQUISTADOR. Yes.

(*Beat.*)

BARBARA. I like it.

CONQUISTADOR. It is not soft like your house.

BARBARA. That's fine.

CONQUISTADOR. Would you like to sit?

(**CONQUISTADOR** *gestures.* **BARBARA** *sits. She looks at him, he looks at her.*)

Are you thirsty?

BARBARA. Yes.

CONQUISTADOR. Wait here.

(**CONQUISTADOR** *disappears. She is alone.*)

BARBARA. (*calling for him*)
¿El Tigre? ¿Pepe?

(**CONQUISTADOR** *appears with two clay cups full of mead and a rolled-up piece of parchment. He sets everything down and sits.*)

CONQUISTADOR. I have something to show you.

(**CONQUISTADOR** *unrolls the parchment. It is a drawing of a* **CONQUISTADOR** *on horseback.*)

BARBARA. A Conquistador. Did you draw that?

CONQUISTADOR. No. It was given to me. Do you want to hear the story?

BARBARA. Is it true? Nevermind, that doesn't even matter. Tell me the story.

CONQUISTADOR. I was out in the fields.

BARBARA. The lush green countryside.

CONQUISTADOR. The fields of the farm. It was planting season.

BARBARA. Of course.

CONQUISTADOR. A shadow fell over me while I bent to the earth. I looked up to see a man dressed as I have never seen a man dressed.

(**GENERAL [ANCIENT]** *appears. He is dressed in a white uniform, a purple sash, white gloves, medals on his chest and sunglasses.*)

I asked him who he was.

GENERAL. General Don Enrique Briz Armengol.

CONQUISTADOR. I asked him where he was from?

GENERAL. Tierra de los Muertos.

CONQUISTADOR. He held out this parchment for me to take. I stood and unrolled it. The sun glowed brown off the earth. I saw this. What is this?

GENERAL. Conquistador.

CONQUISTADOR. And he told me what that meant. He spoke of the New World. Of Savages. Of noble knights on horseback claiming the land from a people destined to be conquered. Of their ladies and their power. I asked him if he was one of them.

GENERAL. No.

(**GENERAL** *walks away.*)

CONQUISTADOR. And then the sun grew big in the sky and his white clothes blinded my eyes. When I could see again, he was gone. I was left alone in the fields with this.

When I returned home that night, I looked at it again. I studied it for hours. Sometimes I could hear the sound in my head of horses' hooves stomping or of victory cries. I could hear fire crackling. I smelled smoke. And when I put my face close, I could see a shape carefully drawn on the helmet.

BARBARA. A tiger.

CONQUISTADOR. Yes.

BARBARA. I used to sit at my desk at work and make lists of cities. Spanish cities. Barcelona, Madrid, San Sebastían: I looked them up, collected pictures. I made a book of the pictures. The cathedrals, the rolling golden hills, people laughing and drinking, playing guitars, dancing flamenco, always lit by fire all around them; people living unafraid of anything, so full of passion and life and –

CONQUISTADOR. Duende!

BARBARA. Duende.

CONQUISTADOR. Burning coals.

BARBARA. Boiling blood.

CONQUISTADOR. Purpose.

BARBARA. Action.

CONQUISTADOR. In my guts.

BARBARA. Down my spine.

CONQUISTADOR. In my center.

BARBARA. In my soul.

(Pause.)

You said I helped you understand yourself. What did you mean?

How did I help you?

CONQUISTADOR. You were a better Conquistador than I ever could be.

You made me remember my true self.

That is who I am now.

(They drink.)

BARBARA. You wanted to sleep with me. Was that as the Conquistador or as you?

(Silence.)

Don't be embarrassed.

CONQUISTADOR. I grew excited when I touched you.

BARBARA. Obviously. It excited me a little, too.

CONQUISTADOR. Truly?

BARBARA. A little. It also disturbed me. I haven't been touched by a man other than my husband in many years. And when he touched me, it wasn't the way that you touched me. Even though his hands were warm and yours were cold.

CONQUISTADOR. I have never been so bold with a woman.

BARBARA. Have you ever been with a woman?

(Silence.)

It's all right.

This drink is good. What is it?

CONQUISTADOR. Mead.

BARBARA. You made it yourself, didn't you?

CONQUISTADOR. Yes.

*(**BARBARA** smiles.)*

What is it? Why are you smiling?

BARBARA. I really like you.

*(Silence. **BARBARA** leans across and kisses **CONQUISTADOR** gently on the lips. She pulls back.)*

Have you ever felt that?

(He bows his head.)

Did it feel good?

CONQUISTADOR. Yes.

BARBARA. You're shivering.

Close your eyes.

(He does. She kisses him again, holding him to her.)

*(The **LAWYER** appears reading off a legal pad.)*

LAWYER. I want faces made of glass, no more soft lips or baby smiles. Sharp angles, gray lines. Eyes like lifeless diamonds. Floating invisible. Barbara?

BARBARA. Go away.

*(**CONQUISTADOR** stops. She pulls him back to her.)*

Not you.

*(**LAWYER** exits.)*

(More kissing, lights dim on them.)

*(**DIVERSION** appears in a separate space in her Flamenco dress, slipping it off as she talks. Underneath she wears a simple white slip. Her tone reflects this.)*

DIVERSION. It was so familiar. Her desire. It was something that I thought had died in me. That I had perhaps killed. And it was dangerous, I knew it was, to be near her, because what if that thing I killed had not died and came back and made me do… something like what she did? It would be so easy. To wake up one morning, take all the money out of the bank, tell Roman to go to hell, buy a plane ticket or a train ticket or just drive away, give up everything I'd decided was important. Find a beach somewhere, steal a horse, ride it along the waves, poor red sangria down my throat while I rode, pour it all over my face.

(She exits.)

BARBARA. Scratchy face.

CONQUISTADOR. What?

BARBARA. Your beard. Scratchy face. It's nice.

CONQUISTADOR. Thank you.

BARBARA. Do you know what to do next?

CONQUISTADOR. Next?

BARBARA. Touch me the way you touched me before.

(**CONQUISTADOR** *does so. They are still.*)

It's different.

(**CONQUISTADOR** *withdraws his hand.* **BARBARA** *takes it and puts it back where it was.*)

It's better.

(**BARBARA** *pulls* **CONQUISTADOR** *down to make love.*)

(**DIVERSION**, *in her slip, rides through on the back of a* **HORSE** *[GUITAR PLAYER]. She surveys the landscape.*)

(*The* **ANCIENT** *appears across the stage with a bottle of sangria, holds it out to* **DIVERSION**, *who rides towards her unquestioningly, like in a dream. She grabs up the bottle and drinks as she rides around and off.*)

(*Lights rise on* **CONQUISTADOR** *and* **BARBARA**, *lying in bed together, entwined peacefully.*)

How do you feel?

CONQUISTADOR. Uhhh…

BARBARA. Good. That's good. You're a man, that's how you're supposed to feel.

CONQUISTADOR. How did it feel to you?

BARBARA. Good. Thank you for asking. You're a wonderful lover.

CONQUISTADOR. I do not remember doing anything.

BARBARA. You responded to everything I did. You cared about me.

CONQUISTADOR. Barbara?

BARBARA. Yes.

CONQUISTADOR. Why did you do this?

BARBARA. Because I wanted to.

CONQUISTADOR. What do we do now?

BARBARA. We lie here like this. You hold me and I feel your warmth around me. We breathe together. We tell each other how lucky we are. We talk about anything, it doesn't matter what. We look into each other's eyes and find peace, amazing peace and relief. You tell me you love my lips. I tell you I love how your arms feel around me. We make plans for the day, or the night, or the next day. We make plans for our life together. We make so many plans.

CONQUISTADOR. You are crying. Are you sad?

BARBARA. No.

CONQUISTADOR. Your husband.

BARBARA. No, it's not him.

CONQUISTADOR. Your husband.

> (**CONQUISTADOR** *is looking at* **JOHN,** *who stands near the bed, simply watching.* **BARBARA** *follows* **CONQUISTADOR***'s gaze.* **JOHN** *wears his blood-stained clothes. He is holding the Spanish sword. He and* **BARBARA** *stare at each other.)*

BARBARA. What are you doing here?

JOHN. I remember the way we started out.

We used to go for long walks holding hands, swinging them. And then I would pull you to me and kiss you and the wind would blow your hair all over your face and I'd brush it away and kiss you again.

And the first time we were naked together and you touched me and you pulled me into you and your lips parted like an O and you sighed so softly.

And the first time you told me you loved me and I loved you.

What is he doing here?

BARBARA. None of your business.

JOHN. Big muscles and no neck.

BARBARA. No.

JOHN. You replaced me with him.

BARBARA. You left me.

JOHN. I'm back.

BARBARA. You're dead.

(**JOHN** *raises the sword.*)

What are you doing? What can you possibly do?

(**JOHN** *quickly stabs* **CONQUISTADOR.**)

No! NO!

CONQUISTADOR. Barbara…

JOHN. Barbara…

(**BARBARA** *grabs the sword away from* **JOHN** *by the blade. She looks at* **CONQUISTADOR**, *who looks up at her. She looks at* **JOHN**, *who sinks to his knees before her and dies.*)

(**BARBARA** *looks at* **CONQUISTADOR**. *He is dying.*)

BARBARA. Please no, not you, no…

CONQUISTADOR. Barbara…

BARBARA. I'm right here, it's okay, you're fine.

CONQUISTADOR. My blood… I am dying.

BARBARA. No, you are not, this can't happen.

CONQUISTADOR. I am going quickly…

BARBARA. No, you can't die!

CONQUISTADOR. The heart of Spain…

BARBARA. No, no, no you don't…

CONQUISTADOR. Red and black and yellow…

BARBARA. Stay with me.

CONQUISATDOR. The New World, the new me…

BARBARA. Please don't leave me.

CONQUISTADOR. *(suddenly very calm, knowing)* Barbara.

(*She looks at him.*)

This is what I was made for.

You have so much…

(*He dies.*)

BARBARA. *(weakly)* Wait…

(He's gone.)

(She holds him.)

(A deep drum pounds offstage. It starts into a rhythmic pattern building in intensity.)

*(Gradually, orange and red light rises upstage. In the light a figure can be made out…. **DIVERSION**. She is naked [literally or gesturally]; holds a long piece of red fabric that she trails behind her.)*

*(**BARBARA** looks at her, cradling **CONQUISTADOR**.)*

*(**DIVERSION** looks back at her.)*

*(**BARBARA** lies **CONQUISTADOR** down gently.)*

*(She stands, not taking her eyes off **DIVERSION**.)*

(She walks towards her.)

*(**DIVERSION** suddenly runs at **BARBARA**, the red cloth flying behind her. She reaches **BARBARA** and starts a wild chaotic dance, using the red cloth in her movement to create swooping, billowing movement, enveloping **BARBARA**. Lights and drumming are very loud. Chaos, bright and disorienting. **BARBARA** stands at the center of it, overwhelmed.)*

(Blackout.)

*(Lights quickly rise tightly on the **ANCIENT**, sitting in a separate space, beating a lone drum with slow intensity. **BARBARA** enters his space, reminiscent of the **CONQUISTADOR**'s first encounter with **ANCIENT**.)*

(She stands before him.)

ANCIENT. Buenas noches.

BARBARA. Good evening.

ANCIENT. Noches.

BARBARA. Night.

ANCIENT. Sí.

BARBARA. Who are you?

(**ANCIENT** *smiles.*)

I don't understand who you are.

(*The* **ANCIENT**'*s smile disappears.*)

I don't understand who I am.

(*The* **ANCIENT** *nods.*)

Can this just stop for second? Can we just hold still for a second?

ANCIENT. Sí.

(*Stillness.*)

(**BARBARA** *looks around the stage.*)

(*Lights have come up.* **DIVERSION**, *wrapped in the red cloth, now stands near the bodies of* **JOHN** *and* **CONQUISTADOR**.)

Do you know who *they* are?

(**BARBARA** *nods.*)

Tell it.

(**BARBARA** *gathers her strength; she goes to* **JOHN**'*s body.*)

BARBARA. This is my husband. His name was John. He played guitar. He used to kiss me on the back of my neck. He would part my hair and press his warm lips…here.

He fell in love with another woman. He fell out of love with me.

(*She takes this in and turns to the body of* **CONQUISTADOR**.)

And this is the Conquistador. His name is Pepe. He kills people. He loves himself. He makes everything up and he makes his own liquor.

BARBARA. *(cont.)* I fell in love with him. I fell out of love with my husband.

They killed each other. I killed both of them.

(ANCIENT beats two heart pulses on his drum. BARBARA turns. DIVERSION has moved to her side. BARBARA looks at her.)

This is Diversion. My best friend, Diversion. She killed her soul. This is her soul.

(ANCIENT beats another heart pulse. BARBARA looks at him.)

This is a textbook. This is the man in charge. This is a lunatic. This is everything I know. This is madness.

(ANCIENT beats the drum again. BARBARA becomes aware of the audience.)

(She takes us in.)

This is a woman alone in her living room. This is a human being alone.

(Silence. BARBARA breathes.)

Can I just be alone? Please? Please.

(BARBARA closes her eyes. The ANCIENT starts a drum roll.)

(DIVERSION disappears.)

(CONQUISTADOR and JOHN rise. They take off the bed together. They bring in the sofa from Act I together and set it where it was. They take off the chairs. They bring on the coffee table. BARBARA keeps her eyes shut. They all leave.)

(BARBARA is alone in her living room. Silence. She looks around.)

(She sits on the sofa. She puts her feet up on the coffee table. She breathes.)

(A doorbell. Silence.)

Come in.

(**DIVERSION** *enters, dressed normally.*)

DIVERSION. Hi.

BARBARA. Hi.

DIVERSION. Are you all right?

BARBARA. Yeah. Sit down here by me.

(**DIVERSION** *does so.*)

Put your feet up on the table.

(**DIVERSION** *does so.*)

DIVERSION. Barbara. Did something happen?

BARBARA. John left.

DIVERSION. What?

BARBARA. John left me for some woman he fell in love with.

DIVERSION. Barbara…

BARBARA. It's all right.

DIVERSION. All right? He left you. Aren't you devastated?

BARBARA. No.

DIVERSION. But you're all alone. It's terrible.

BARBARA. I'm going to take a trip.

DIVERSION. Spain?

BARBARA. Yes.

DIVERSION. You don't speak Spanish.

BARBARA. I'll learn.

(*Blackout.*)

End of Play

Saltimbanques

SALTIMBANQUES was first produced at Yale University in New Haven, Connecticut in Artspace from April 18-25, 1998. The performance was directed by Christopher W. White, with sets by Cathy Braasch, lights by Matt O'Neill, costumes by Sara Hume, sound by Jed Roher. The Production Manager was Fell Ogden. The cast was as follows:

JAMES . . . . Steven Klein
LOUISE . . . . Anne Martin
DEBORAH . . . . .Kim-Thu Posnett
MOMMY . . . . Amy Herzog
PAUL . . . . .Ben Vershbow

SALTIMBANQUES subsequently underwent several revisions through various workshops from 1999-2004, particularly with directors Keven Moriarty and Tim Farrell, culminating in a staged reading on March 29-30, 2004 at Playwrights Horizons, produced by NascentWorks, and directed by Tim Farrell. The cast was as follows:

JAMES . . . . Scott Blumenthal
LOUISE . . . . .Colleen Werthmann
DEBORAH . . . . Mia Barron
MOMMY . . . . .Lois Markle
PAUL . . . . .John Wellmann

CHARACTERS

JAMES – (30s) Brother
LOUISE – (30s) Sister
DEBORAH – (30s) Ex-Girlfriend
MOMMY – (40-60s) Crazy artist
PAUL – (30-40s) Lost

SETTING

In the present: a cabin interior, a nearby park, a hotel room.
In a fluid and overlapping past: artist studios, apartments, a hospital
room, art galleries.

TIME

1998 or so.

AUTHOR'S NOTES

The play frequently asks for a confluence of actual and imagined
realities. Stage directions describe how to do this and where actors
should imagine themselves individually, even in the midst of more
expressionist surroundings.

Prologue

(**MOMMY**, *a woman of indeterminate age, stands with* **PAUL** *at an easel. She watches him paint, his teacher. Then startles him.*)

MOMMY. A family in a field.

PAUL. Huh?

MOMMY. A boy, a girl, is this their mother?

PAUL. I don't know, maybe.

MOMMY. It looks familiar.

PAUL. It's just an image I had in my mind.

MOMMY. Who is he, this man here?

PAUL. Um…a family friend?

MOMMY. There is no right or wrong answer. I am only curious.

Is he not the woman's husband?

PAUL. No, I don't think so.

MOMMY. The children are not his?

PAUL. They might be.

MOMMY. I like where this is going. It is mysterious. It makes me imagine all of their lives and loves. Perhaps the man and woman loved each other in Paris under a skylight in a thunderstorm while the rain turned to hail and broke through in a million cubes of glass.

PAUL. I hadn't thought of that.

MOMMY. Yes, but I did. And isn't that the beauty of all this.

PAUL. All this?

MOMMY. Creation. Imagination. This boy and girl.

PAUL. Yes? What do you imagine about them?

MOMMY. What do *you* imagine about them?

PAUL. *(thinks)* Twins.

MOMMY. Good.

PAUL. It's funny, most of my art teachers just comment on my technique.

MOMMY. Would you prefer I commented on your technique?

PAUL. No. No, I appreciate how you do it much more.

(*Silence.* **MOMMY** *looks at* **PAUL** *with great interest. She looks at the painting.*)

MOMMY. It reminds me of something. Shall I tell you what?

(*A dramatic burst of thunder. Lights fall them.*)

ACT I.

BLUE

*(A cabin in the woods. It is raining outside. **JAMES**, 30, stands looking at a portrait of himself resting on the floor, propped up where he and the audience can see it. In it, he is a good-looking teenager. Currently, he looks like shit. **LOUISE**, 30, bursts in wearing a raincoat, drenched. **JAMES** is not startled. He turns to her casually. They take each other in.)*

JAMES. You found me.

LOUISE. I knew where to look.

You look awful.

JAMES. Thanks. So do you.

LOUISE. What have you been doing here?

JAMES. Standing. Sitting. I was just looking at your portrait.

*(**LOUISE** looks at it.)*

LOUISE. I called Deborah. She told me you left. I didn't believe her at first, but then she was crying.

JAMES. Have my eyes always looked like that? They look like his eyes.

LOUISE. Are you on something?

You're shivering.

JAMES. You left the door open.

*(**LOUISE** closes the door behind her.)*

LOUISE. Can you start a fire?

JAMES. I tried. I failed.

LOUISE. City boy.

JAMES. Mommy always did it for us.

(**LOUISE** *grabs a couple logs and starts making a fire.*)

LOUISE. *I* always did it for us. Your memories are twisted.

(*She squats down and gets to work.*)

JAMES. I love you.

LOUISE. Are you drunk?

JAMES. No. A little.

LOUISE. I love you too, James.

JAMES. I'm standing here and I don't know what to do with my body. I smell the pine trees. I hear the rain.

LOUISE. *(snap out of it)* Come on, James.

JAMES. I remember everything. She used to start the fire, then she taught you. Why do you think she never taught me?

LOUISE. She wanted you helpless.

JAMES. I'm not helpless.

LOUISE. No, of course not, you're a big success. I'm helpless. You just don't know what to do with your body.

JAMES. I feel like I haven't seen you in years.

LOUISE. Weeks.

JAMES. Three weeks since the funeral.

LOUISE. Yeah.

JAMES. Do you ever look at yourself? Since she said it. Look in a mirror, see him in your face. Or look at one of his paintings. The Boy Leading His Horse. I see myself in that now.

LOUISE. That's a painting, not a mirror.

JAMES. He always painted himself.

LOUISE. *(stopping her work, realizing)* I should take you out of here. This is the last place you should be.

JAMES. Why?

LOUISE. You know why.

(*Silence.*)

JAMES. She was crying? Deborah?

LOUISE. Yes. *(beat)* I'm proud of you for leaving her.

JAMES. I think I'm still in love with her.

LOUISE. That'll pass.

> *(***JAMES*** *turns away.* ***DEBORAH*** *walks on dressed for Soho. She throws a white shroud over* ***LOUISE*** *where she kneels, making her into a sculpture.* ***JAMES*** *looks at the sculpture. A gallery.)*

DEBORAH. Do you like it?

JAMES. Yes.

DEBORAH. What do you like about art?

JAMES. What?

DEBORAH. What do you like about it?

JAMES. I feel it. It hits me in the gut. Do you know the artist?

DEBORAH. I am the artist.

JAMES. Oh, I should have known. James.

DEBORAH. I know who you are, James Bourbon. You're the hot young dealer. I'm the hot young sculptor. Wanna discover me?

> *(***JAMES*** *laughs.)*

You have pillow eyes. I like your laugh.

JAMES. Are you always this bold?

DEBORAH. I'm insecure, I'm covering. You said you liked it.

JAMES. I love it.

> *(***DEBORAH*** *kisses* ***JAMES*** *good on the mouth, then exits, taking the shroud with her. Lights snap back to cabin.)*

LOUISE. Leaving her was the smartest thing you ever did.

JAMES. It still hurts.

LOUISE. I know.

JAMES. I have a big hole in my chest.

LOUISE. I'm sure you do.

JAMES. Have you ever felt that? Isn't it strange that I don't even know if you've ever felt that?

LOUISE. I've felt that.

JAMES. Sometimes I feel like I don't know anything about you.

LOUISE. You know some things.

JAMES. I used to. I used to know everything when we were kids.

LOUISE. Not everything.

JAMES. You're so angry all the time.

LOUISE. Why aren't you?

JAMES. I have no reason to be angry.

LOUISE. You have many.

(JAMES *turns away.*)

JAMES. It's possible, you know. I did the math. She was in Spain at the right time. She had that picture to prove it. The picture with her and the matador.

LOUISE. That picture could have been Coney Island. It isn't possible. It's a story, just another story.

JAMES. She never claimed anyone else was our father.

LOUISE. We don't want him to be our father. He was a bastard.

JAMES. So are we. And he was the greatest artist of the Twentieth Century.

LOUISE. He was not our father.

(**MOMMY** *is revealed upstage, lying on a hospital bed. A hospital room.*)

MOMMY. James.

Come here, James, I have something to tell you and your sister.

(**JAMES** *walks over to* **MOMMY.**)

Louise, I need you, too.

(**LOUISE** *does not move, but looks at* **MOMMY.**)

It's time I told you about your father.

LOUISE. You don't know who he is.

MOMMY. Well, that isn't actually true. It's time you knew.

LOUISE. Please don't.

MOMMY. I've waited so long because I didn't want your lives to be hindered by the knowledge. But now you are ready and I am about to die.

JAMES. Mommy…

MOMMY. It's all right, James. It will be. His name was –

LOUISE. No…

MOMMY. Pablo Picasso.

(An overly dramatic burst of thunder.)

LOUISE. I'm leaving.

MOMMY. This is the truth, Lou.

LOUISE. Of course, Mommy, it's always the truth. I'll be back later. James, will you be here?

JAMES. Picasso?

MOMMY. Yes.

LOUISE. I can't take this anymore.

*(**LOUISE** walks off.)*

MOMMY. How is Deborah, James? Is she afraid of me?

JAMES. What?

MOMMY. You must be careful with her. Careful with yourself. So many things can go wrong.

JAMES. I can't…can we go back to what you just said?

MOMMY. Oh, you're in shock. I'm sorry. Yes, Pablo was your father.

*(Back to the cabin with just **JAMES** and **LOUISE**.)*

LOUISE. Even if he was our father, so what? He's dead. And if he were alive, he wouldn't exactly be there for us, would he? So he might as well not be our father even if he were, which he isn't.

JAMES. But he might be.

LOUISE. Why is it so important?

JAMES. Are you kidding?

LOUISE. I don't need it or want it in my life. Why do you?

JAMES. *Our father!* We came from somewhere. We never knew where we came from.

LOUISE. I always assumed we were the products of Mommy's imagination.

(**JAMES** *is silent.*)

It makes my skin crawl.

JAMES. But you admit it might be possible.

LOUISE. It's also possible we were the postman's kids.

JAMES. We're not the postman's kids.

LOUISE. I don't know, James. I did the math and it seems like there was always a postman around.

JAMES. She said it so clearly. All the details. There was clarity like there never was before.

(**LOUISE** *shivers.*)

What.

LOUISE. I wonder if you'd be so excited about it if she had just told us he was some guy she met in a bar, some real human being somewhere. Some failure. Would it matter so much to you?

JAMES. Yes.

LOUISE. Then how come it never mattered before?

JAMES. Maybe it's all I have left now.

LOUISE. Then I guess you don't need me.

(**LOUISE** *starts to go.*)

JAMES. Wait. Don't. Please.

(*She turns back to him.*)

When I was leaving, I had your portrait under my arm; it was the only thing I took. When I was leaving, Deborah was opening the refrigerator and she pulled out an orange and she said: Are you okay? And I said: Yes. Like when we were kids in separate bedrooms saying "Are you okay?" and the other one says yes and then we'd both ask Mommy and she'd say yes.

LOUISE. You're having a breakdown.

JAMES. Do you remember how we asked each other then? How we were all so close to each other?

LOUISE. Our memories are different.

JAMES. Are you okay, Louise?

LOUISE. Never been better.

JAMES. I don't believe you.

LOUISE. Well, look who's talking.

JAMES. I need you to stay.

LOUISE. I will. I need you not to say that some ridiculous fantasy is the only thing you have left when I'm standing in the room with you.

JAMES. I'm sorry.

(**JAMES** *sits.* **LOUISE** *sits.*)

LOUISE. It was the only thing you took with you?

JAMES. It was the only thing that meant anything to me. I wish you still painted.

LOUISE. Sorry, I don't.

JAMES. I was remembering your moons before you came.

LOUISE. How sweet.

JAMES. There were seven, right? In perfect squares. From just a sliver to all the way full by the sixth and in the seventh it explodes into a sun.

LOUISE. That wasn't a sun, it was exploding into nothingness.

JAMES. It looked like a sun.

LOUISE. If there was an eighth square you would have seen a big black hole.

JAMES. What a way to go out.

LOUISE. With a pretentious college moon painting? Yeah, big finish.

JAMES. You stopped out of spite. Out of fear of being anything like her.

LOUISE. Wrong. I quit because that's exactly how I felt. Like those paintings. I had nothing more to paint. And I will never be like her in a million years!

(**JAMES** *shrinks back.*)

And that's where we get when we talk about me.

But we're not here to talk about me. You're the subject. You're the one who just escaped from something. You're the one who needs help.

JAMES. You're the one who ran after me.

Why did you have to do that?

LOUISE. Because you were free from her grip and I could finally get to you. And I knew you finally needed me.

JAMES. Whose grip?

LOUISE. Deborah, James. The Marquise de Psycho.

(**DEBORAH** *walks in with a colorful trapazoidal mask and a leather jacket. She drops the mask over* **LOUISE**'s *face and leads* **JAMES** *to a different space. Their apartment. She hands* **JAMES** *the jacket; he puts it on. A game.*)

DEBORAH. Cigarette. Left inside pocket.

(**JAMES** *reaches into the jacket pocket and pulls out a pack of cigarettes. He takes two, hands one to* **DEBORAH** *without looking at her, puts one in his mouth.*)

Lighter.

(**JAMES** *pulls a lighter. Lights* **DEBORAH**, *them himself, replaces the lighter.*)

Look at me, James.

(*He does.*)

You're beautiful like that. Take a drag for me. So beautiful. The smoke frames you. And your leather jacket. You're a rock and roll demon. You're a black leather lizard. I'm your iron cross lover. We walk like we want a fight. Like we're hard and tough. Together we're solid granite. Are you with me?

JAMES. *(enjoying it)* Yes.

DEBORAH. How much money did you make today?

JAMES. *(momentarily out of it)* What?

DEBORAH. How much money did you make today, topaz goliath?

JAMES. I –

(returning to form)

made ten thousand dollars today.

DEBORAH. Easy money for you.

JAMES. Two phone calls.

DEBORAH. What did you sell, Lord Bourbon?

JAMES. Rogerson collage.

DEBORAH. You look like James Dean to me.

JAMES. One of his best works.

DEBORAH. You're a movie star in black and white, in a night club, in a bar; your face glows and sweats in the light.

JAMES. Sold it to a stock broker.

DEBORAH. The clicka your heels, you shoot pool, roll dice –

JAMES. A Wall Street tycoon.

DEBORAH. You dance with your hips low and your shoulders back.

JAMES. He had no idea what he was buying.

DEBORAH. Stud for sale on your forehead –

JAMES. *(sadly)* Or appreciation.

DEBORAH. And I buy you up and take you home.

JAMES. Deborah.

DEBORAH. Your turn.

JAMES. Deb?

DEBORAH. Sterile statue minx-face god.

JAMES. Debbie.

DEBORAH. Your turn!

JAMES. *Deborah.*

DEBORAH. What.

JAMES. The cigarette is giving me a headache.

(*Silence.*)

DEBORAH. (*genuinely surprised*) You want to stop?

JAMES. Or maybe start over but with no cigarette.

DEBORAH. All right. Put it out. Take off the jacket.

(*He does both.*)

You're not in the mood.

JAMES. No, it's just…

DEBORAH. That's fine, it's all right. I was just trying to have fun.

JAMES. I was having fun, too. I just got distracted.

DEBORAH. Did it seriously bother you that somebody bought something without appreciating it? Is that what distracted you?

JAMES. Maybe. Mainly the headache.

DEBORAH. You're an art dealer, why should you care?

JAMES. Because it's…you know, it's art.

DEBORAH. It's money. It's a job. And this was supposed to be foreplay.

(**JAMES** *looks at her; he quickly starts to put the jacket back on.*)

JAMES. You're right. Here, start again. I'll do it better.

DEBORAH. No, forget it. It's too late. I'm making you compromise your ideals.

JAMES. Start again.

DEBORAH. I'm not in the mood anymore.

(*She strips the jacket off him.*)

Shall I make us some drinks?

JAMES. Deb…

DEBORAH. It bothers me, too. I'm an artist, of course it bothers me. I just deal with it in a different way.

JAMES. I know.

DEBORAH. My little sensitive art dealer.

I'll get us drinks. And then I want to sketch you some for the sculpture. Would that be better?

JAMES. Yes.

DEBORAH. I love looking at you. Knowing you're mine.

You should tell me when I'm going too far.

JAMES. Never. I like being yours. I want you like you are.

DEBORAH. I can't wait to start sculpting you.

(**JAMES** *smiles with some awareness.*)

I'll be in the kitchen. Making our drinks. Naked.

(*She kisses him and exits, taking the jacket with her.* **MOMMY** *appears standing upstage with an IV drip.*)

MOMMY. I met him after the bullfight.

(**JAMES** *exits after* **DEBORAH**, *unaware of* **MOMMY**.)

He was there in the stands, smoking a cigarette, his white shirt and bare legs in the sun. He shook my hand. Firm. His lips brushed my cheek, his stubble. He was magnetic, he pulled me in. And so virile, like the bulls they killed in his honor. Eighty years old, a living myth, the most alive man I'd ever met. I told him I was an artist, too. Would he like to see some of my work?

LOUISE. (*from under the mask, though unaware of it*) Mommy, you didn't really meet him.

MOMMY. I did a lot more than meet him.

LOUISE. You make things up.

MOMMY. I tell you my life. I've seen some amazing things, I tell you my life.

LOUISE. Sure you do.

MOMMY. James appreciates me.

LOUISE. James has problems.

MOMMY. It's because you're the older child.

LOUISE. By two minutes, Mommy.

MOMMY. A lot can happen in two minutes. In two minutes, they shot our President in the head and the whole world heard about it. I was standing there watching the parade. For me, it happened in two seconds.

LOUISE. Uh-huh…

MOMMY. I'm going to be dead soon. Earth cover my head and dirt in my mouth. My eyes will pop, my cheeks will suck in. But I don't feel like being burnt up; I'm in the mood to rot.

LOUISE. Jesus Christ…

MOMMY. Do you want to hear about this or do you want to hear about your father?

LOUISE. Neither.

MOMMY. Where is James?

LOUISE. He's with Deborah.

MOMMY. Oh yes, of course he is. Blue room weeping.

(**DEBORAH** *enters, leading* **JAMES** *behind her, blindfolded. She is showing* **JAMES** *the sculpture,* **LOUISE** *in her mask.*)

DEBORAH. Ready?

JAMES. Ready.

(**DEBORAH** *removes the blindfold. Silence.* **JAMES** *cannot speak. He goes to the sculpture and touches it.*)

DEBORAH. You hate it.

JAMES. No! No. I just – it's weird to see…

DEBORAH. You.

JAMES. Yes.

DEBORAH. Is that you?

JAMES. Yes. Isn't it?

DEBORAH. Does it look like you to you?

JAMES. I think so. I just look so…

DEBORAH. Lonely.

JAMES. No.

DEBORAH. Sad. Trapped.

JAMES. I wouldn't say…

DEBORAH. That's all right. Those are my big themes. This is what I do. In art. In my relationships. When I combine them. This is what you get.

(beat)

Are you sure you want this?

JAMES. What are you talking about?

DEBORAH. I consume things, people. It's in my nature. I'm a killer. I'm killing you.

JAMES. Deborah.

DEBORAH. What.

JAMES. Is this another game?

DEBORAH. Usually. Are you up to playing it?

JAMES. I don't understand.

DEBORAH. I love you. I want to eat you. You've fallen into my web. *(beat, a realization)* I love you. Usually there's no love involved. I'm not supposed to care about you like I do.

(indicating the sculpture)

It's supposed to end there.

JAMES. What's supposed to end?

DEBORAH. The game.

(She looks at him.)

I don't fall in love, that's not what I do.

JAMES. I'm in love with you.

DEBORAH. I know. That's always a given. It's the reciprocation thing that's got me all…confused.

Why do you love me?

JAMES. Because you're everything I need.

MOMMY. A woman on a red bull's back. Flying over a Christmas town. Her factory girl's handkerchief waving, her knees clutching tight to the bull. Do you like it, James?

JAMES. I love it.

DEBORAH. Why do you need me?

MOMMY. It's just a sketch now. It's going to be the size of a wall.

JAMES. I like the bull.

MOMMY. Do you like it, Louise? No, you probably think it's a mess.

DEBORAH. Am I like her?

JAMES. Like who?

MOMMY. James likes messes.

DEBORAH. Your mother.

(**LOUISE** *hurls the mask from her face.*)

LOUISE. JAMES!

(**DEBORAH** *and* **MOMMY** *scatter. Back in the cabin.*)

JAMES. I'm right here.

LOUISE. No, you're not. You keep turning catatonic.

JAMES. I haven't slept.

LOUISE. For how long?

JAMES. Two days.

When I sleep I have dreams.

LOUISE. What kind of dreams.

JAMES. Everything swirled around and all mixed up. People and animals and masks and death. I see what death looks like. Red nothing. Lightning. It's terrifying.

LOUISE. You should try to sleep again. I'll be here with you.

JAMES. You artists.

LOUISE. What?

JAMES. When you have dreams like this you can paint them. You can get them out of you. The rest of us can't. I watched Deborah, I watched Mommy, I watched you. You could hold me spellbound the way you could turn a blank canvas into a living thing.

LOUISE. You're talking about someone who isn't me anymore.

JAMES. Deborah used to come up with these ideas. In the middle of the night, she'd say:

(**DEBORAH** *is lit separately;* **JAMES** *and* **LOUISE***'s scene goes on as she speaks.*)

DEBORAH. I want to build a melting igloo on the ground. With Eskimo bones and coats poking out of it.

I'm thinking of a giant ship that's caught inside a whale's mouth. And the whale is made of glass.

I want to make a sculpture of you where instead of arms you have ladders and monkeys are crawling up the ladders.

LOUISE. Those are pretty weird fuckin' ideas, James.

JAMES. Yeah, but she could make them happen. Visualize it here and then create it. Like you. You could have this concept you wanted to express and you could express it. And Mommy.

LOUISE. Ah-ha, what about Mommy? We never did see that painting that was the size of a wall, did we?

JAMES. Doesn't matter. The sketch was good enough.

LOUISE. Some of us artists get stuck between our ideas and expressing them. And what comes out isn't what we wanted at all. And it's never finished. And it tortures us. And that's much worse than bad dreams, believe me.

JAMES. You always hated Deborah's sculptures.

LOUISE. Yeah.

JAMES. Why?

LOUISE. They were cruel and sadistic. Just like her.

JAMES. She wasn't sadistic. She didn't mean to be.

She really loved me.

You don't believe me.

LOUISE. She loved herself. She saw you as part of her for a while. That's what she loved.

JAMES. What the hell do you know?

LOUISE. I know what I saw. I know I've met people just like her.

JAMES. Artists?

LOUISE. Yeah, mainly. Fuckin' artists. Forget artists.

JAMES. I can't.

I miss her, Louise.

LOUISE. You'll get over her.

JAMES. No. Mommy. I miss Mommy.

She should be here. This was our little cabin together. Everywhere I look I see her.

LOUISE. That's why I think we should leave.

JAMES. I don't want to leave yet. I want to deal with this. I need to deal with this. Don't you?

LOUISE. I have been dealing with this. For a long time.

JAMES. You didn't hate her, did you? Mommy. No matter what you said?

LOUISE. I never said I hated her.

(JAMES *raises an eyebrow.*)

She made me angry.

JAMES. But you loved her.

LOUISE. Yeah, I loved her.

JAMES. We should have been there together at the end, the three of us.

LOUISE. Yeah.

JAMES. What did she say?

LOUISE. When?

JAMES. Then. At the end. I know she would have said something. She would have had last words.

LOUISE. She said she was proud of us. I told you.

JAMES. She would have said something more.

LOUISE. She didn't. That was it. No deathbed revelation.

Sorry. I told you exactly how it went.

(*A knock on the door. They both look at it.*)

Who else knows you're here?

JAMES. No one.

(JAMES *walks to the door and opens it. A* **POSTMAN** *[PAUL] with a huge beard and a small package enters.*)

POSTMAN. Good afternoon.

JAMES. Afternoon.

POSTMAN. Are you James Bourbon?

JAMES. Yes.

POSTMAN. This is your package.

JAMES. I don't understand.

POSTMAN. Somebody mailed it to you.

JAMES. No one knows I'm here.

POSTMAN. Are you sure you're James Bourbon?

JAMES. Yes.

POSTMAN. Somebody knows you're here.

> (**POSTMAN** *hands him the package.* **JAMES** *looks at it, confused.*)

Good afternoon.

> (**POSTMAN** *exits.*)

LOUISE. Are you going to open it? I don't think you should.

> (**JAMES** *opens it quickly and pulls out a skull, painted half red and half blue.*)

What the hell is that? Put it back in the box.

(He does. He pulls out a rose that has been cut to fit in the box.)

A rose? Put that back, too.

Who sent that? Deborah.

JAMES. I never told her about this place.

LOUISE. But who would send something like that?

JAMES. Red and blue.

LOUISE. I don't even know how to think about this.

JAMES. Red to Blue. A rose. Rose and blue.

Blue to Rose.

LOUISE. What?

JAMES. It's a puzzle.

LOUISE. It's a cadavre! Blue to Rose?

JAMES. Like Picasso.

LOUISE. Oh no.

JAMES. Blue Period to Rose Period. Like the painting. In the museum. When you went with me after she said it.

LOUISE. You're kidding me.

(Lights swing swiftly to **ART MUSEUM TOUR GUIDE** *[***POSTMAN***]. Still with the enormous beard. Now with a white button down shirt and a name tag.* **LOUISE** *and* **JAMES** *turn to look at him. They are all in an art museum.)*

GUIDE. You've found my favorite. We've only recently acquired it. "Meditation" or "Contemplation" depending on your translation. Do you know it? Do you know its significance? Do you know it's the transitional work? Because, of course, he had his Blue Period in 1903-04 and he was lonely and sad and alienated and, well, blue, and then there was his Rose Period directly following…the harlequin families…boys and horses and so on. Rosy, earthy, right? Maybe still a little lonely, but warmer and human, right? Filled with the spirit, the, uh, the spirit of him, his environment, his changing life. And Meditation is the transition from Blue to Rose. Just look at it. You see his first major love interest who was not a prostitute, and she's lying there asleep bathed in yellow light. And there's the artist (he's put himself in as usual, you see) and he's watching her sleep, right? And he's dressed in all blue and there's the blue ink spilling on his desk. But the wall in back of him, look, it's rosy. It's red, it's earthy. And this whole thing is about the blue bleeding out of him. This is where it happens. Why? You're lookin' at her. So is he.

Her name is Fernande Olivier. She's so beautiful, she's serene. Look at his face. You see? How he's affected. What she does to him. Is he calm? Is he filled with love and longing? Is he even just a little resentful? Or all of these. What the hell is her presence doing to him? You follow me? He keeps her in his apartment. She doesn't have shoes in the winter so she's stuck there. Trapped. He's got her, he's transfixed, the great transition is coming.

(The sound of knocking. **DEBORAH** *has slipped on, wearing a party dress.)*

DEBORAH. Hold on a minute, I'll be right there!

*(***GUIDE*** disappears.* **JAMES** *moves off.* **LOUISE** *goes to* **DEBORAH***'s implied front door, having knocked on it.)*

Louise, what a pleasant surprise.

LOUISE. I was in the neighborhood.

DEBORAH. Yes, you look wonderful.

LOUISE. Is James here?

DEBORAH. James? He's asleep actually. Zonked out.

LOUISE. Oh. I thought I would stop by and say hi. You know, I was in the neighborhood…

DEBORAH. Well I could wake him up if you want.

LOUISE. Am I interrupting you? From work?

DEBORAH. Work? Oh, my hands. No, that's left over blood. It's so hard to wash out. I'm getting dressed for a party.

LOUISE. Blood?

DEBORAH. Yes. Well it was dirt and blood, the dirt washed off. I was commissioned to do another Living Log for the Thompson Gallery.

LOUISE. Huh.

DEBORAH. Do you want me to wake him up for you? He's been feeling sick

LOUISE. He's sick?

DEBORAH. Yes, he hasn't been feeling well. It's nothing serious. He's had some trouble sleeping. Digesting. His digestion isn't so good. Do you want me to wake him up?

(silence)

LOUISE. No.

DEBORAH. Are you sure?

LOUISE. Yeah. Yeah, I'll just call later. Again. Will he be up this evening do you think?

DEBORAH. We're going to a party.

LOUISE. Tonight?

DEBORAH. Yes.

LOUISE. Do you think that's a good idea?

DEBORAH. It's a gallery party.

LOUISE. Maybe you should go by yourself. If James is feeling sick.

DEBORAH. He'll be all right.

(beat)

LOUISE. Why don't you wake James up for me.

DEBORAH. I thought you –

LOUISE. I changed my mind. I want to speak to him.

(beat)

DEBORAH. I don't think I should wake him up. He really should sleep.

*(**LOUISE** stares daggers.)*

LOUISE. Are you going to tell him I was here ?

DEBORAH. Would you like me to –

LOUISE. Yes, that's why I asked.

DEBORAH. I'll tell him you came by.

LOUISE. And to call me.

DEBORAH. I'll tell him to call you.

LOUISE. Will you?

DEBORAH. Yes.

LOUISE. Tell him *as soon as he wakes up to call me.*

*(**LOUISE** turns to go.)*

DEBORAH. Louise?

Do you think we'll ever be friends?

LOUISE. Are you at all interested in being my friend?

DEBORAH. We have a lot in common.

LOUISE. Do *I* make *you* physically ill?

DEBORAH. No.

LOUISE. Huh.

(**LOUISE** *turns again.*)

DEBORAH. Louise. I was very sorry to hear about your mother.

(**LOUISE** *heads for* **DEBORAH** *like she actually might kill her. Instead she shouts into her apartment.*)

LOUISE. JAMES! I know you're listening! CALL ME!

(**LOUISE** *exits.* **DEBORAH** *closes her door.* **JAMES** *enters in a blue party shirt.*)

JAMES. Did you say something?

DEBORAH. There was someone at the door. You didn't hear him?

JAMES. No.

DEBORAH. Salesman. I told him to get lost.

JAMES. Are you ready soon?

DEBORAH. Would you zip this up for me?

(**JAMES** *goes to her. He starts to zip her up from the back. He zips down. He reaches in under her dress. Not mean:*)

What are you doing? This won't make things better.

JAMES. I know.

(*He pulls her dress off. Lights go to* **MOMMY,** *standing with the IV drip and speaking out as before.*)

MOMMY. She was his first real love. Fernande Olivier. They met in a thunderstorm, in front of their building in Paris. He was holding a cat, blocking the door, teasing her, flirting. He lets her in. He shows her all of his sad blue paintings. She is overwhelmed by his talent and good looks. As they make love she opens her eyes to see a painting of a loin-clothed man with a naked woman hanging from his neck.

A tragic Madonna with a blue baby stands nearby. Everyone looks like they've been weeping. And Fernande weeps in his arms. And he weeps in hers. This is the purest moment they'll ever share.

Of course, I'm jealous of her. He was poor then. Poverty makes a person a better lover.

(**PAUL,** *clean-shaven and dressed as a jester, walks on arm-in-arm with* **DEBORAH**. **MOMMY** *fades. A gallery party.*)

PAUL. But the best lovers of all are the ones who don't give a shit and make it their business. Same goes for artists.

DEBORAH. Do you really believe that?

PAUL. No, do you?

DEBORAH. James, James. There he is.

(**JAMES** *walks in.*)

Paul, this is James. James, Paul. Paul is a truly amazing artist. You are, aren't you, Paul? You must be, look at the way you're dressed. James is a wonderful dealer. My little dealer. You should speak to each other.

PAUL. I know who Mr. Bourbon is.

DEBORAH. Of course you do.

PAUL. I mean besides your reputation. I knew your mother, God bless her. I'm very sorry she died.

JAMES. Thank you. How did you –

PAUL. I was in a class she taught years ago. I was her favorite pupil.

JAMES. Really?

PAUL. Of course I never met you or your sister. You must have been kids then.

DEBORAH. My god, how old are you, Paul?

PAUL. Older than I look. I have a youthful spirit. But James – I'm going to start calling you James now, how do you feel about that?

JAMES. I don't have any feelings about that.

PAUL. James, your mother was a very special woman. Amazing. I'm sure you know that.

JAMES. Yes.

PAUL. And I'm not just talking about her art. I mean her mind and soul. I used to stay for hours after class and just talk to her. The things she told me. The things she's done. Well, I'm sure you know, they are…

JAMES. Amazing.

PAUL. Astounding.

(silence)

DEBORAH. What do you think of Paul's outfit, James?

JAMES. It's ah –

DEBORAH. He's a clown.

JAMES. Yes.

PAUL. I thought it was appropriate for the occasion.

DEBORAH. I've invited Paul for drinks and dinner sometime.

JAMES. All right.

PAUL. You're not a very big talker, are you, James? Surprising given the lineage.

JAMES. I'm very tired.

DEBORAH. He's been terribly busy all week.

PAUL. I understand. Believe me. I'm very familiar with exhaustion. Your sister's an artist, too, isn't she?

JAMES. She hasn't painted since college. How did you know that?

PAUL. Your mother told me. Oh shit, look, there's someone I have to talk to over there. Will you excuse me for a moment? I really want to continue this conversation.

DEBORAH. Of course. Go on, Paul.

PAUL. So good to meet you.

*(**PAUL** shakes **JAMES**' hand and walks off.)*

DEBORAH. You don't like him.

JAMES. I – uh…no, I don't think so.

DEBORAH. I don't like him either.

JAMES. You invited him over for drinks and dinner sometime.

DEBORAH. That was just to be nice. He won't actually come.

JAMES. I'd like to get out of here.

DEBORAH. What's wrong?

JAMES. I feel a little sick.

DEBORAH. Shouldn't you shmooze some more?

JAMES. I'm too worn out to shmooze.

DEBORAH. I've been talking you up to everyone.

JAMES. I appreciate it.

DEBORAH. We should stay for a while longer.

JAMES. Why?

DEBORAH. James. This is our world. This is what we do. We can't just leave because we're tired.

(beat)

JAMES. Maybe I'll leave by myself.

DEBORAH. Don't be ridiculous. I'll go snag Paul and bring him back here. Why don't you get a drink for yourself.

*(**LOUISE** walks in angrily dialing on a portable phone. Lights shift to kill the party. **DEBORAH** steps downstage.)*

Hello?

LOUISE. Let me talk to my brother you fucking bitch!

DEBORAH. He's not here.

LOUISE. Bullshit! Give me my goddamn brother!

DEBORAH. He left.

LOUISE. I don't believe you.

DEBORAH. He left me. He left for good. He's not here anymore.

LOUISE. He left you.

DEBORAH. Yes. He finally left me. Are you happy?

LOUISE. No.

*(Lights and action return to the cabin. **DEBORAH** fades. **JAMES** returns, dressed for present time.)*

JAMES. Louise, talk to me.

LOUISE. We shouldn't be here. Will you please let me take you somewhere else?

JAMES. Why?

LOUISE. Too many ghosts. And now this thing. Everything is too much here.

(A knock on the door.)

Oh Jesus. Don't. Don't answer it.

*(***JAMES*** goes to the door. The ***POSTMAN***.)*

POSTMAN. Louise Bourbon?

LOUISE. Close the door.

POSTMAN. I found this at the bottom of my bag. I missed it the first time.

*(He holds out a thick envelope. ***JAMES*** takes it.)*

LOUISE. What the fuck is this?

POSTMAN. Have a good day now.

*(He walks off. ***JAMES*** closes the door. He holds the envelope out for ***LOUISE***. She shakes her head no. He opens it and pulls out a paintbrush.)*

LOUISE. It's her. It's Mommy. She set this up somehow before she died.

JAMES. Agua.

*(***LOUISE*** looks at him bewildered.)*

On the paintbrush. Someone wrote it on. "Agua."

(He holds it out to her. She'll have none of it. He starts off.)

LOUISE. Where are you going?!

JAMES. Get some water.

*(***LOUISE*** follows him off. Lights shift to ***MOMMY*** and ***PAUL*** standing over an easel, thirteen years younger than usual. They both wear loose colorful rags. ***PAUL*** has just painted something. ***MOMMY*** looks at it over his shoulder.)*

MOMMY. Saltimbanques.

PAUL. Huh?

MOMMY. What you've done here. Your subject matter.

PAUL. Saltimbanques. As in…

MOMMY. Acrobats. Vagabonds. Circus families. Harlequins in rags.

PAUL. Like Picasso.

MOMMY. Yes.

PAUL. I didn't mean to imitate. I wasn't even thinking…

MOMMY. No, Paul, I'm not accusing you of imitating. Your styles are very different. He's looser and freer. You're more uptight.

PAUL. Oh?

MOMMY. That's your style. Don't be ashamed of it.

PAUL. Okay.

MOMMY. It's interesting. What you do. I've told you that before. You shouldn't change it. It's also interesting to see him creeping in there. It fascinates me. I don't know what Pablo would say. Probably something dirty.

PAUL. It really…it fascinates you?

MOMMY. It would fascinate him, too.

PAUL. That means a lot to me if it fascinates you, if you like it.

MOMMY. I do.

PAUL. Because I feel I've learned so much from you. You've given me so much, and I admire you. Very greatly admire.

MOMMY. Thank you, Paul.

PAUL. Is that wrong to say?

MOMMY. No. I don't think I deserve such praise.

PAUL. You deserve everything.

MOMMY. Paul, that's very sweet of you.

PAUL. I'm in love with you.

  (*Silence.* **MOMMY** *looks at* **PAUL** *with great interest.*)

MOMMY. I knew it.

PAUL. Oh God, did I just say that?

MOMMY. Of course you said that.

PAUL. I really should not have said that.

MOMMY. I could sense it from when I first saw you.

PAUL. I should probably leave now.

MOMMY. And when I saw this, I was almost sure.

PAUL. Saw what?

MOMMY. Your painting, of course. I knew.

PAUL. You knew from my painting?

MOMMY. Saltimbanques. That's what he told me was his favorite. You'd think it would be something wilder, something cubist. But his soul was in the Rosy Saltimbanques.

PAUL. I don't – what?

MOMMY. He told me in the hotel bed. After we made love and bathed.

PAUL. Huh?

MOMMY. And when he left he said we would meet again. Then he died months later and I thought it was the end. Except for the kids. I thought that was the end of that. My brush with true greatness. But obviously…

PAUL. What are you talking about?

(*beat*)

MOMMY. You have no idea, do you? He wouldn't let you know. Typical.

PAUL. Who? What…

MOMMY. Pablo.

PAUL. I'm –

MOMMY. That's right.

PAUL. I don't understand what you're saying.

MOMMY. Pablo.

PAUL. *Pablo.*

MOMMY. Pablo Picasso died and his spirit found your young artist body to inhabit. Because he wasn't finished. He had more to do. And he had to find me. You're not in love with me Paul, he is. He's using you. But you don't mind because you're young and you'll sleep with anything. I know a good hotel we can go to, Pablo. I'll take Paul there and we can make love again.

PAUL. What are you talking about?!

MOMMY. Pablo, tell him.

PAUL. STOP! This is a joke. You're making fun of me.

MOMMY. No. Pablo, it's time you told the boy.

PAUL. What are you saying?

(Silence. **MOMMY** *smiles at* **PAUL.***)*

MOMMY. Call for help.

PAUL. What?

MOMMY. I won't remember any of this. Call for help, Paul.

PAUL. I don't need help.

MOMMY. I'm going to need help. I'm about to have a seizure and a psychotic episode. I hope you'll visit me and remind me of what I said. Paul – I hope you'll – Goddammit! Oh, there it is. Salt in the bank.

*(***MOMMY*** drops to the ground* **PAUL** *is horrified. He runs out calling for help. Cabin lighting.* **JAMES** *walks on holding a cup of water, followed by* **LOUISE***. He takes the brush and dips it in the water. He picks up the skull and brushes it all over with water. Then he brushes on a specific area. He holds it up for* **LOUISE** *to see. She is silent, then looks at him.)*

LOUISE. Yo llegaré. Prepárate.

JAMES. What does it mean?

LOUISE. I'm coming. Prepare for me. Who the hell is this freak?

JAMES. It isn't Mommy.

LOUISE. I'm getting you out of here.

JAMES. No.

*(***LOUISE*** grabs the skull and brush from* **JAMES***, gets rid of them, and yanks him towards the door.)*

LOUISE. Come on, we're going.

JAMES. No, Louise!

LOUISE. Yes, James!

> (**LOUISE** *uses all her strength to pull* **JAMES** *out the door, slamming it behind her. Lights rise slowly on the platform, staying on the cabin, too.* **MOMMY** *rises. She steps off the platform. She looks around the cabin, apparently happy to be back in it. She looks at the sunset. She turns and picks up the skull. She brings its teeth to her lips for a kiss. Blackout.)*

ACT II.

ROSE

(DEBORAH *and* JAMES *tornado onstage in their underwear, a blanket swirling with them, landing on the floor, rolling around, making love.*)

DEBORAH. James, James, James…

JAMES. I'm right here…

DEBORAH. You're some kind of angel. Kiss me there. There. There. My silver angel. Your touch, every touch so soft.

(*not stopping*)

When do you think you're going to leave me?

JAMES. Huh?

DEBORAH. Don't stop. When do you think you're going to save yourself from me?

JAMES. Save myself from…

DEBORAH. Yes. Yes…

JAMES. I don't have to save myself.

DEBORAH. Of course you do. Don't stop.

JAMES. You're not… I'm not…

DEBORAH. You are. I am. I just want to know when. So I can be ready.

You stopped.

JAMES. We're in the middle of…why do you have to…

DEBORAH. Because I'm evil. And you're destroying yourself by being with me.

(*Silence. Another blanket tornadoes on stage.* PAUL *and* MOMMY, *much more dressed than* JAMES *and*

DEBORAH, *fly this one. They and their blanket land directly on top of* **JAMES** *and* **DEBORAH**.)

PAUL. You said you would forget.

MOMMY. Usually I do. Only goes to show…

PAUL. I've never made love to a much older woman.

MOMMY. It's only appropriate, Pablo. You were eighty. Virile, but eighty.

PAUL. I should tell you something.

MOMMY. I haven't given you a chance. Go on, talk. I'm ready.

PAUL. I don't believe I'm possessed by Picasso's spirit. I'm just lonely and enamored of you.

MOMMY. That's fine for you to believe, Paul. It must be traumatic, dealing with possession.

PAUL. I haven't been with a woman since a couple years ago. I've been…

MOMMY. Consumed with your work, I understand. I haven't been with a man for seventeen.

PAUL. I don't know why I came to you like I did except out of pathetic carnal and emotional need. I swore I wouldn't go near you after your seizure.

MOMMY. You came to me because *he* wanted me again. It's all right if you don't understand that, you don't have to.

PAUL. I'm not Pablo Picasso.

(**JAMES** *stands abruptly, disturbing the heap. The two scenes are alive but retain their split.*)

MOMMY/DEBORAH. James.

PAUL. What?

MOMMY. You should meet James and Louise.

DEBORAH. Where are you going?

PAUL. Who?

MOMMY. Your kids.

JAMES. I don't know.

MOMMY. They don't know yet. I haven't told them.

DEBORAH. I ruin everything.

(*JAMES is silent.* **PAUL** *stands.*)

PAUL. I don't have kids.

MOMMY. You have kids all over the place; these are your twins.

(**PAUL** *starts to exit.* **DEBORAH** *reaches out to* **JAMES**. *He does not reach back to her.*)

I need some water.

(**PAUL** *exits.*)

DEBORAH. I ruin everything.

(**DEBORAH** *exits.* **JAMES** *looks to* **MOMMY**. *She looks back kindly at him. She rises, back in her scene and looks towards where* **PAUL** *left, exiting after him.*)

MOMMY. Paul…

(**LOUISE** *enters. Lights shift back to present time, now outside.* **LOUISE** *takes* **JAMES** *to the blankets.*)

LOUISE. How's this spot?

JAMES. It's all right.

LOUISE. Do you want to go somewhere else?

JAMES. No.

(*He straightens the blankets out to sit on.*)

It's like where she used to take us. The old picnic spot.

LOUISE. This is a highway rest stop, James. She took us to the woods.

JAMES. We should have brought Champagne and pork rinds.

(**LOUISE** *laughs, stops.*)

LOUISE. Yeah, we were real Bohemians. Trust fund Bohemians.

JAMES. Always gotta get a dig in, don't you.

LOUISE. We're not staying here for long, just until we figure out where we're going next.

JAMES. Yes, ma'am.

LOUISE. I thought you liked being ordered around.

(JAMES *stares at her.*)

I had to take you out of the cabin. It wasn't safe.

JAMES. Who do you think it is?

LOUISE. I don't know and I don't care as long as it doesn't follow us.

JAMES. It could be his ghost. Picasso.

(*She gives him the "you're kidding me" look.*)

Do you have a better explanation?

LOUISE. You're using Mommy-logic.

When in doubt, the most far-fetched ridiculous thing must be the answer.

JAMES. You're scared. I know you are and I know why. Because it might be true.

LOUISE. Picasso's ghost?

JAMES. We're his kids! It's possible! Admit it. It might be true.

LOUISE. True? True like Mommy and the revolution? True like Mommy and the days she spent with the nomadic camel riders? How 'bout the time she sailed across the ocean on that fishing boat with the whaler who bore a striking resemblance to Captain Ahab? They are stories, James. It's one big story; that was her life. Now we have our lives.

You have your gallery parties and I have my mundane everyday miserable existence. That's what's true. Everything else is fantasy or gross speculation.

JAMES. What the hell is wrong with you?

LOUISE. Do you really want to know? Do you really want to know anything about me?

JAMES. Yes!

LOUISE. It's not romantic, James. There are no flying bulls or famous dead people with me.

JAMES. I know.

LOUISE. Go ahead, ask something.

JAMES. What's it like where you work?

LOUISE. It's like a big gray beehive. We all sit in our cubicles and look at the postcards we've pinned up on our dividers.

JAMES. You've said you like it sometimes.

LOUISE. It's better than food service, but it's pretty boring.

JAMES. Have you ever been in love with someone? I mean I know about those guys you dated in college. But really in love?

LOUISE. Yeah.

JAMES. What's his name? When did it happen?

LOUISE. It's been a while. And it's not just one. And it's not a him.

JAMES. You mean you…

LOUISE. Yes, I like women.

JAMES. Why didn't I know that?

LOUISE. Because I didn't tell you and you never asked.

JAMES. You were away for so long. And then you came back and…

LOUISE. And you were with Deborah and Mommy was getting sick.

I wanted to tell you a lot of things since I came back.

JAMES. Why didn't you?

LOUISE. Deborah wouldn't let me near you.

JAMES. That's not true. We talked. It wasn't like we never talked.

LOUISE. I didn't tell you things because I didn't want you to tell Mommy. And she was in the hospital and you saw her every day so you would have. I didn't want her to know anything about my life.

JAMES. I wouldn't have told her if you didn't want me to.

LOUISE. You would have told her. She would have found out. And then she would have incorporated everything from my life into her mythology. You know she would've. I can hear her – I was a lesbian when I was with Gertrude Stein, Lou. She was a fortune teller and she said someday I'd have a lesbian daughter and –

JAMES. I get the point.

LOUISE. I wanted my own life. Alone.

JAMES. It was because she was your mother. You reject her because she was supposed to be your role model.

LOUISE. You sound like bad therapy. You think that's why I'm a lesbian, too?

JAMES. No.

LOUISE. I don't need any more bad therapy, James. I've had plenty thanks to our childhoods.

JAMES. It wasn't that bad. We were taken care of.

LOUISE. *You* were taken care of. I took care of her. Remember? No, you wouldn't. That was behind the scenes. You were protected from that part.

JAMES. You're a real martyr.

LOUISE. I cared for her every single day. I lived with her insanity hovering over my head. I had to be sane, to comfort her, to do the practical things she was incapable of doing – no, not even incapable, things she could refuse to do once I was around to do them. You'll never know.

JAMES. And what would your psychiatrists say about me?

(*beat*)

LOUISE. Oedipal complex, except you want to resurrect your father instead of killing him. And you can't define yourself except through someone else's eyes.

JAMES. Nice.

LOUISE. I could do Deborah, too, if you like.

JAMES. Why stop now, you're on roll.

LOUISE. Deborah was her own fantasy and she gave you a fantasy just like Mommy, only you could have sex with her.

JAMES. Go to hell.

LOUISE. You sound angry, James.

JAMES. Who do you think you are?

LOUISE. You're definitely angry now.

JAMES. Don't try to manipulate me.

LOUISE. Why not, everyone else does?

JAMES. Goddammit Louise, you self-righteous…shithead.

LOUISE. Oh yeah, get mad at me, I deserve it…

JAMES. All your negative crap.

LOUISE. Uh-huh…

JAMES. That's all you ever did with your stupid exploding moons and putting me down because I could feel things and you were cold. Angry bitter cold nasty thing and you want everyone to feel sorry for you because you had to grow up too fast. Everyone has to grow up too fast! What do you think I did? You think I was a child because I found joy in what Mommy said, because I dared to entertain that some of the things she told us actually happened? Who else believed her? You? Anyone? I'm the one who made her life worth living and for some fucked-up reason you're the one who got to be with her when she died.

LOUISE. You couldn't have taken that and you know it.

JAMES. I don't know that and you don't know shit.

LOUISE. Yep, that sums it up, good closure, James.

JAMES. I'm the one who's a success at what I do. You're the one who quit. Don't tell me anything.

(beat)

You said it first.

LOUISE. I needed you.

JAMES. I was there.

LOUISE. You were not there! Shut up. Don't talk. Do you know that day? That day I came to see you and your mommy-substitute kept me from you, lied to me right in my face and I know you heard every single word…

JAMES. Stop…

LOUISE. I needed you then more than I ever needed anything in my life. *Desperately* needed you. And where were you?

JAMES. How am I supposed to know when you need me or not when most of the time you've got this huge wall up?

LOUISE. You heard me at door. I was begging you to come out.

JAMES. Why? Why then all the sudden?

LOUISE. Because I had a lead weight around my neck. Because I had to talk to you. I had to tell you something.

JAMES. What did you have to tell me?

LOUISE. Everything she said… She said…all of it… She said…

(She can't finish; she screams with frustration, looks up)

Why did you have to do this to me?! Why did you have to leave me with this?!

JAMES. Louise?

LOUISE. *(back to* JAMES, *fast and furious)* And then Deborah slammed the door in my face and I went down in the elevator, spit at my reflection in the mirrors, ran outside in the cold air, down to the corner, into the drug store, bought the pack of razor blades, they saw it in my face what I wanted – too terrified to stop me; got on the subway – head humming, face hot, fists clenched tight on the metal bars, looking at everyone else like I could kill – got home, walked in my door, to my bathroom, stood there right over the sink with the blades –

JAMES. No…

LOUISE. Picture it, James. Here's some truth for you. Me standing in front of my bathroom mirror looking at myself with a razor blade poised over my wrist. Have you ever looked at yourself like that? I felt so stupid and pathetic and I looked at the whole pack and thought it was funny I had to buy a whole pack when I only really needed one and I pressed the sharp point against my skin and a red drop popped out. And then I was throwing up on my knees and crying and rubbing my hands on the cold tiles just to feel something. The ridges. The blood on the white floor, little stripes. Little useless meaningless stupid lines.

*(Silence. **JAMES** takes her wrist, looks at it. He pulls her to him roughly and holds her tightly. Silence.)*

James, I can't breathe. James.

JAMES. *(still holding her tightly)* I made you do that?

LOUISE. No.

JAMES. I did. I heard you. I was hiding.

LOUISE. You couldn't have known.

JAMES. I knew it was important. I was only thinking about myself. I knew you needed me. Please, please forgive me. Oh my God, I almost lost you.

LOUISE. You didn't.

*(**JAMES** lets go his hold and looks at her.)*

JAMES. Please don't ever… Please. Forgive me. You're the only person in my life. If you had…if I lost you…

LOUISE. I didn't do it. It's okay. I forgive you.

(Silence. They breathe and look at each other.)

JAMES. Can I tell you something?

LOUISE. No, you should definitely hold back now.

JAMES. I like the idea of knowing who my father is.

*(Silence. **LOUISE** looks at him)*

For me. Knowing my father.

LOUISE. I know. I understand. I do. I just don't want it to be Picasso. That's too much to take.

JAMES. Why?

LOUISE. Because I'll never measure up to that. I'll never come anywhere near that.

All it does is make me sad. Do you understand that?

JAMES. Yes. I needed to hear that.

LOUISE. Is there anything else you need to hear?

(**JAMES** *takes her hand again.*)

JAMES. What was it she said? In the end. What you needed to tell me. What did she say?

(*the sound of twigs snapping*)

LOUISE. Did you hear that?

JAMES. What.

(*more snapping*)

LOUISE. That bush. What is it?

JAMES. Maybe it's just some animal.

(*shaking of leaves*)

LOUISE. Oh Jesus…

(*A blinding shaft of lights shoots down on* **JAMES** *and* **LOUISE.** *Both shut their eyes and reach for each other. A wild and overpowering drumming.* **DEBORAH** *and* **PAUL** *run out dressed like Saltimbanques. They swirl in threatening circles around* **JAMES** *and* **LOUISE,** *like animals and crazed evil acrobats. The effect is disorienting, weird and threatening. The lights go crazy, the drums get wilder,* **PAUL** *and* **DEBORAH** *get more frantic. The frenzy builds to a terrible climax then drops suddenly. Blackout and silence. Lights rise on* **MOMMY** *standing alone dressed in her harlequin rags. We are in her head when she is having a seizure.*)

MOMMY. Feeling of dread. Of impending, no stopping it again it comes this is warning but too late to change much. Living in fear is waste, better to forget. Accept it when it is inevitable, deny it when it is lying in wait. Static like not moving or like white light, it is both. I feel like I've been through wars. Not like a soldier but like a survivor and I am. From this Cuban Revolution over to Spain and how the horns tear into the flesh and lift the fighter off the ground – he is so shocked, feels no pain even, but is just amazed at his flight and his similarity to a skewered piece of pork. Shady shaky grimace and then all the color bleeds out until he's black and white. Static again and divided in grids like Kahnweiler. All angles in time at once the only way is division careful at first then comes more freedom.

Pills do no good and asylums are wasted and dull. Better to live and feel.

You're an artist, be creative.

(**MOMMY** *collapses. Lights shift.* **DEBORAH** *and* **JAMES'** *place.* **DEBORAH, JAMES,** *and a newly arrived* **PAUL. LOUISE** *is now rolled up in the blankets, a sculpture on the floor.*)

PAUL. Is this your stuff all over, Deborah?

DEBORAH. Yes, mostly.

PAUL. It's good stuff. Isn't it, James?

JAMES. Yes, absolutely.

DEBORAH. I think we're both a little surprised that…ah…

PAUL. That I came without warning. Yes, I tend to be surprising that way. This was the day you mentioned for dinner though, wasn't it?

(**JAMES** *shoots* **DEBORAH** *a look.*)

DEBORAH. Yes, I suppose it was. It's just that usually someone coming to dinner –

PAUL. Calls first, sure. I understand. The problem is I don't really have a working phone right now. A friend borrowed it for a performance art piece.

DEBORAH. Huh.

(**PAUL** *notices* **LOUISE** *in the blanket.*)

PAUL. This. I like this very much. It's yours, right?

DEBORAH. It's something I'm working on.

PAUL. What do you call it?

DEBORAH. Pig in a blanket.

PAUL. But it's definitely not a pig, is it?

DEBORAH. It's a woman.

PAUL. So there's a statement.

DEBORAH. You could say that.

PAUL. I completely get it. What do you think, James?

JAMES. *(having paid no attention)* Yeah?

PAUL. What do you think?

JAMES. Um. Are you planning on staying for dinner? We were actually going out tonight, weren't we, Deb?

PAUL. I'm sorry. I'm intruding. I thought I was invited. It's a misunderstanding, my fault entirely. I feel terrible.

DEBORAH. No, Paul, it's all right. It's all right, isn't it, James?

JAMES. What's all right?

DEBORAH. We did invite you for dinner. Please stay and join us. We'll all go out.

(**JAMES** *starts to walk away.*)

PAUL. Wonderful. You're my kind of people. And if you like afterwards, we can go back to my studio and I'll give you a tour. It's modeled after your mother's, James. You'll see how I learned from her.

(**JAMES** *looks at* **PAUL.**)

She taught me everything I know. You should see the effect she had on me.

JAMES. The effect she's had on you?

PAUL. She changed my life. Yours too, I imagine.

DEBORAH. So it's all decided. Dinner then art. Right James?

JAMES. Right.

(**JAMES** *abruptly walks out.*)

DEBORAH. You'll have to forgive James. Sometimes he gets moody. Funny, isn't it, the two artists in the room are the normal ones.

PAUL. He doesn't like me very much, does he?

DEBORAH. No.

PAUL. I don't make a good first impression. I grow on people.

(PAUL and DEBORAH exit. Lights change, MOMMY enters in a bathrobe. She rushes to LOUISE and lies beside her. LOUISE is a little girl in her bed.)

MOMMY. LOU! Lou!

LOUISE. Mmm? Huh?

MOMMY. Lou baby…

LOUISE. *(half-asleep)* Mommy?

MOMMY. Yes, sweetie, it's Mommy. I'm here.

LOUISE. Huh?

MOMMY. I'm here, baby, I'm not going anywhere.

LOUISE. What, Mommy?

MOMMY. I just – I'm sorry I woke you up, sweetie Lou. You're so precious.

LOUISE. Are you okay, Mommy?

MOMMY. I had a terrible dream. I dreamt the tanks came back and took me away this time. And you and Jamie were all alone.

LOUISE. Tanks?

MOMMY. And then I saw you in the street and you were in danger and I wanted to save you but I couldn't move.

LOUISE. Mommy, I don't know what you mean.

MOMMY. I dreamt the tanks came back and the revolution was crushed.

LOUISE. Revolution. Oh.

MOMMY. Mommy's told you about the revolution.

LOUISE. Uh-huh.

MOMMY. They took us away in box cars.

LOUISE. Yes, Mommy.

MOMMY. I'm so glad you're safe.

LOUISE. Do you need to sleep next to me again?

(silence)

MOMMY. Yes.

(MOMMY snuggles up next to LOUISE.)

Thank you, sweetie.

LOUISE. It's okay, Mommy.

> (**MOMMY** *and* **LOUISE** *shut their eyes. The drums from earlier start to sneak back in.* **PAUL** *enters. He wears a matador's jacket and sash. He holds a sword. His gaze falls on* **MOMMY.** **LOUISE,** *to him, does not exist. He begins to approach* **MOMMY** *as if she were a bull. He slowly brings the sword up, prepared to thrust down as he walks towards her.*)

MOMMY. Paul.

> (*He freezes. She has opened her eyes, seeing neither the sword nor his stance.*)

PAUL. Yes.

MOMMY. I haven't told the children about their father. I'm waiting until I know I'm going to die. I feel that's the right way.

> (**PAUL** *has not yet put the sword down.*)

I've decided they shouldn't know yet. They're not ready to know yet. It's important that they discover their own identities first. But, Paul, after I die, after I've told them, I want you to tell them who you are. Do you understand?

PAUL. Who I am?

MOMMY. You know who you are.

PAUL. I don't. I can't tell what's real about me.

MOMMY. You're divided.

> (*Silence.* **PAUL** *brings the sword to rest safely at his side.*)

PAUL. Yes.

MOMMY. Because there are two of you. And you've only just discovered that.

PAUL. I don't know what I've discovered.

MOMMY. I've discovered it for you; you're still adjusting to it.

PAUL. I don't think I should see you anymore.

MOMMY. That's right. That's part of it. You will not see me anymore. You have to go off on your own now. Just keep your ears open. You need to be ready when I go. You have to tell your children.

PAUL. How would I ever tell them this?

MOMMY. You're an artist. Be creative.

LOUISE. *(still as a little girl)* Mommy, you're squeezing too tight, I can't sleep.

MOMMY. *(still in **PAUL**'s scene)* Don't fail me, Paul.

(silence)

PAUL. I won't.

*(**PAUL** exits.)*

LOUISE. Mommy, I can barely breathe.

*(**MOMMY** gets up and exits. **JAMES** and **DEBORAH** walk back on. **LOUISE** returns to being a sculpture.)*

DEBORAH. He grows on you, doesn't he?

JAMES. Like a fungus.

DEBORAH. I think I like him very much.

JAMES. Great.

DEBORAH. What the hell is wrong with you?

JAMES. Nothing.

DEBORAH. James.

JAMES. Nothing's wrong. If you like him, I'm glad.

DEBORAH. Are you?

JAMES. Yes.

DEBORAH. You might not want to be.

JAMES. Why?

DEBORAH. Because I want to suggest we have an affair with him.

JAMES. What?

DEBORAH. I mean I've been missing my life the way it used to be and I want to have a ménage á trois again.

JAMES. Are you serious?

DEBORAH. I think Paul would be interested. I think it's something you should at least try.

(silence)

JAMES. I think you're going too far.

DEBORAH. Huh?

JAMES. You told me to tell you when.

DEBORAH. You said you wanted me like I am.

JAMES. Are you trying to push me away, is that what this is?

DEBORAH. Maybe. Is it working?

*(Silence. **JAMES** looks intently into **DEBORAH***'s eyes.)*

What are you trying to find when you look at me like that.

This is what being with me is like. If you're not going to leave me, you have to accept this.

JAMES. Why do you have to do this?

DEBORAH. It's who I am. It's who I really am, James.

I'm sorry.

Why don't you just leave me?

JAMES. I don't know how.

DEBORAH. Yes you do.

*(**LOUISE** scrambles out of her blanket to stand. She walks to **JAMES** takes his hand and walks him away from **DEBORAH** as if she weren't there. **DEBORAH** exits.)*

LOUISE. James.

JAMES. I know.

LOUISE. She went peacefully. Like going to sleep.

JAMES. Did she say anything?

(beat)

LOUISE. No.

JAMES. I knew I should have stayed.

LOUISE. You couldn't have known.

JAMES. I can't believe it.

LOUISE. Me neither.

Are you okay?

JAMES. No. My mother just died.

(beat)

You?

LOUISE. Same.

JAMES. Louise…what did she say?

*(**MOMMY** enters. She picks up and folds the blankets as she talks.)*

MOMMY. Kids, I have to talk to you. You're teenagers. You're going to head out into the world soon, I want to tell you about the world you're heading out into. I'm sure you think you know what to expect. The truth is you'll never know. You don't know what's going to happen in the next five minutes. A man in a mask could easily burst in, kill us, gut us and eat us. That's an extreme example, but you just never know. So what I'm telling you is: be careful. Don't plan too far into anything you can't get out of – because you don't want to be trapped. Adaptability is everything. James, do you understand?

JAMES. Yes.

MOMMY. Louise?

LOUISE. Sure.

MOMMY. And also you should make sure to help each other. You're her only brother; you're his only sister. You're twins. You balance each other. Don't forget that, it's important.

LOUISE. Is that it, Mommy? I have to get back to my painting.

MOMMY. That's all.

*(**LOUISE** turns to go.)*

Louise?

LOUISE. Yeah?

MOMMY. I'm glad you're a painter.

(beat)

LOUISE. Thanks.

(**LOUISE** *walks off.*)

MOMMY. Are you all right, James?

JAMES. I get scared.

MOMMY. What do you get scared of?

JAMES. The future.

MOMMY. You need to learn how to live in the moment. Have you started reading the Camus I gave you?

JAMES. No.

MOMMY. I wish I could give you my book. It says many of the same things.

JAMES. I wish you could, too.

MOMMY. But that's a good example of what I mean. You never know when the publishing house and bookstores will be raided. You never know when someone's going to take your book and burn it. And you have to start over but all you've got left is what's in your head. Maybe *you* should write a book, James.

JAMES. I couldn't.

MOMMY. Why not?

JAMES. I'm not a writer.

MOMMY. That never stopped me. Everyone's a writer.

But you're scared. That's all right, baby. Maybe that'll change tomorrow.

(**MOMMY** *hands* **JAMES** *the blanket and kisses him on the cheek.*)

I'll read your book when you write it.

(**MOMMY** *smiles at* **JAMES**, **JAMES** *smiles back. She exits.* **JAMES** *spreads the blanket out like it was for the present time scene with* **LOUISE**. *As he does this,* **PAUL** *enters. He hold the red and blue skull in his hands. He is finishing up the red coat with a paint brush.* **JAMES** *is unaware of* **PAUL**.)

PAUL. They go from town to town in their rags and bright tights. Sometimes a girl will balance a ball while a strong man lifts a dumbbell. Sometimes they walk the high wire. Or walk on their hands. They are acrobats. They are surrounded by a crowd of onlookers. They perform their routines. They get lonely in their heads.

You never know how creativity will manifest itself. When I paint them. Their interchangeable faces. Never an honest smile or real touch. Except to lift and flip and tumble down.

(*PAUL squats down. The sound of twigs snapping. Lights flash down on JAMES and LOUISE as before, back in present time.*)

LOUISE. Did you hear that?

JAMES. What.

(*more snapping*)

LOUISE. That bush. What is it?

JAMES. Maybe it's just some animal.

(*shaking of leaves*)

LOUISE. Oh Jesus…

JAMES. Maybe it's a raccoon.

(*PAUL is revealed trying to flee. He stops when he sees that they see him. Silence.*)

PAUL. Oh shit.

LOUISE. Who are you?

PAUL. I'm…

LOUISE. Who the hell are you and what do you want from us?!

JAMES. Paul.

LOUISE. Paul? Who's Paul?

PAUL. Nobody. I'm not Paul.

I'm…Pablo Picasso. I'm your father.

LOUISE. What?

PAUL. Your mother told me to do it. She said I was… I'm Pablo Picasso, I'm your father. I don't know what comes next. I'm possessed. Oh Christ.

JAMES. Our mother?

PAUL. She knew it because my painting was…derivative.

(**PAUL** *starts laughing.*)

And I was in love with her. And she said it wasn't me it was Pablo, and I didn't really believe her at first, but then she got inside of me. He got inside of me. Everybody's inside me and I'm possessed. Can I just be your father? I've wasted my whole life for you and you never even knew me. Hi. I'm Paul. I'm a big fat phony bullshit crock of shit lunatic. And I love you both very much.

LOUISE. James?

JAMES. Our mother told you…

PAUL. She said: be creative. So I tried to be creative. I tried to give you hints. I thought it was the right thing to do. Make it mysterious. Because it's supernatural.

LOUISE. How the hell did you know our mother?

JAMES. He was her student.

PAUL. She taught me everything I know.

I don't know anything.

JAMES. Deborah introduced me to him. He came to our house for dinner. I couldn't stand him.

PAUL. I was trying to figure out how to talk to you.

LOUISE. When did he know her?

PAUL. You were kids. You were at school.

LOUISE. My God.

JAMES. She told you Pablo Picasso was our father when we were kids?

PAUL. She said to wait until she died to tell you.

LOUISE. How many years ago?

PAUL. Thirteen. I've been waiting. I had to wait all this time.

JAMES. Louise?

LOUISE. I know. But it doesn't mean anything. He said he was possessed for Christsakes.

JAMES. She knew. She waited. She never did that before, it's different from everything.

(**LOUISE** *stares at* **PAUL,** *then at* **JAMES.**)

LOUISE. I don't even know how to think about this.

(*blackout*)

Meditation

(The cabin, **JAMES** *and* **DEBORAH**'s *and a hospital room.* **JAMES** *is being painted by* **LOUISE** *and sketched by* **DEBORAH**, *each in her own space.* **PAUL** *sits cross-legged on the floor of the cabin.* **MOMMY** *lies in her hospital bed.)*

PAUL. I used to love it so much. Painting. I would lose myself in it. And I thought I was finding myself, too. You know?

LOUISE. Yeah.

DEBORAH. James, could you turn your head more towards me?

LOUISE. Could you look over here a little more, James?

PAUL. I loved watching her work, your mother. There's something about the way a woman like her paints. So powerful. Like a magician or a god.

JAMES. She was like a god.

LOUISE. She was only a woman.

DEBORAH. I'd like you to take your shirt off now.

*(***JAMES*** takes off his shirt.)*

LOUISE. What are you doing, James?

JAMES. Taking off my shirt. I'm hot. Is that all right?

LOUISE. Sure. If it makes you more comfortable.

DEBORAH. The hardest part about you is the gentleness of your neck.

LOUISE. I was really only painting your face.

DEBORAH. The place where your neck meets your shoulder. There's something so delicate about you. I remember the first time I saw you naked. You were so fragile.

LOUISE. Turn your head a little more towards me.

*(***JAMES*** does so.)*

DEBORAH. That's when I really knew. How deeply I felt about you. And it is so deep. You know, James? I feel so much when it comes to you. Sometimes it's too much and I do the wrong things and I end up hurting you. I have to be so careful. Like you were a child or made out of thin glass.

I imagine you like that sometimes. Little red shorts. Skinny legs, knobby knees. Maybe a scar from falling or accidentally running into something. Because you have less control over your body when you're younger. You're barefoot on a hot sidewalk. You have a cute blue shirt. Maybe you have a little boy belly poking out. And your small shoulders. Your chin. Your face. Your hands. Tiny nose. Soft cheeks. And smooth, smooth hair on your head. Your baby head in the sun. I want to hold you like that sometimes. I think how much simpler we'd be if we didn't have to be lovers. If I could just love you like a grown-up loves a child and you could love me like a little boy loves a pretty woman in a nice dress. I'd just have to resist eating you all up.

LOUISE. James?

JAMES. Mm.

LOUISE. There's a tear on your cheek.

JAMES. Yeah.

LOUISE. We should stop for a little while.

DEBORAH. I think we should take a break. I need a drink. Do you want one?

LOUISE. Can I get you a glass of water or a tissue? I'll get you a tissue.

JAMES. No. That's all right. I'll get it myself.

(**JAMES** *exits.* **LOUISE** *and* **DEBORAH** *watch him go. Their eyes meet in the middle.*)

MOMMY. Lou. There you are, Louise.

(**LOUISE** *turns to* **MOMMY.** **DEBORAH** *walks off.* **LOUISE** *goes to* **MOMMY.** *In the hospital.*)

Where's James?

LOUISE. He's at work.

MOMMY. Too bad.

LOUISE. He'll come by after.

MOMMY. It'll be too late.

LOUISE. Mommy, don't talk like that.

MOMMY. I can feel it happening. It's happening right now.

LOUISE. What's happening?

MOMMY. Draining away. It's too fast.

LOUISE. You're gonna be fine, Mommy.

MOMMY. I will be fine. I'll be dead. That's the way it works. And it will be fine.

LOUISE. Not yet, Mommy.

MOMMY. I'm afraid so, baby. I'm afraid so. You're seeing me off right now. I was going to try to wait until I had both of you. I just can't. I can't.

LOUISE. No.

MOMMY. It's going to be beautiful, Lou, beautiful. I've never felt such…clarity. Truly. Clarity in my mind. I am fully here, Louise, like I've never been. That's how I know. Look at me. Look at my face relax. Come closer.

(**LOUISE** *does.*)

I'll tell you something now because I can. I'll tell you but you can't tell James.

I know what's real and what's not. I know what's made up. And it's almost everything. Almost. And I know you know, which is why I can tell you. These weren't lies, Louise. They were how I wanted to live. You want to live a certain way, you make it happen one way or another. Do you see?

But you can't tell James. But you can know that I had this beautiful moment of peace when all the blur, all the dizziness disappeared. When I lay on this bed and looked at you and told you this is the end and I am aware of it and of who I am. Do you see? Do you see? Louise. There's a revolution in my head, baby. My baby, there are heroes and bullfights here. And that's where they belong. That's where I want them. Hold my hand.

(**LOUISE** *does.*)

I see into the future. I see everything I never thought I'd see. I see you beside me. I feel your hand. I'm so happy you're an artist. I'm so proud. Don't tell James. He doesn't have anything else.

(**MOMMY** *dies. Silence.* **LOUISE** *stands with her.*)

PAUL. I'm not Picasso. I'm not an artist. I'm not a student. I'm not a lover. I only know what I'm not.

LOUISE. Mommy…

PAUL. I met a family of artists. I met a brother and sister in the woods. I almost recognized myself. The one who made me like this was dead. And the one I was supposed to be. And I had to figure out who I was without them.

LOUISE. Please, Mommy. Please. I'm not ready for this.

(**DEBORAH** *enters in her bathrobe. She walks to a real or implied refrigerator door and opens it.* **JAMES** *enters,* **LOUISE**'s *first portrait under his arm. She looks at him with awareness. He stops and looks at her.*)

DEBORAH. Are you all right?

JAMES. Yes.

(**DEBORAH** *takes her hand off the refrigerator.*)

DEBORAH. I'm going to miss you.

JAMES. I'll miss you, too.

DEBORAH. You're blessed, James. Someone's protecting you. You're going to be fine.

(**JAMES** *and* **DEBORAH** *smile sadly at each other.* **JAMES** *goes to* **LOUISE**'s *new painting. He takes it off the easel to look at it. He is at peace. He shows it to* **DEBORAH**. *She nods approvingly.*)

LOUISE. (*still squeezing* **MOMMY**'s *hand*) It's only just started, you see. All that's there are the eyes and the shape of the face.

JAMES. The eyes.

LOUISE. Are you going to say you have his eyes?

JAMES. No, I have yours. And hers. And mine.

PAUL. Could he really have been your father?

JAMES. It doesn't really matter.

LOUISE. We might as well say he was.

    (**JAMES** *looks at her. Smiles.*)

JAMES. No one would ever believe us.

PAUL. I would.

JAMES. Louise. Tell me what she said.

LOUISE. She said it was all true, especially the parts that never happened. She said she was proud I was an artist. She said she was so happy you loved art. She said she tried the best she could. She said you have to make the life you want for yourself one way or another.

    (*silence*)

JAMES. Thank you.

PAUL. Now what?

LOUISE. Now we live the rest of our lives.

    (*Blackout. End of play.*)

Green Man

GREEN MAN received its West Coast premiere at STAGEStheatre (Amanda DeMaio and Patti Cumby, producers) in Fullerton, California on June 26, 2015. The performance was directed by Jeremy Lewis. The assistant director was Ani Marderosian and the stage manager was Claire Carrigan, with sets by Jon Gaw and Kristin Campbell, lights/sound by Harrison Haug, costumes by Christina Perez, and make-up by Laura Young. The cast was as follows:

ABIGAIL . . . . Miriam Ani
RONALD . . . . Chris Hayhurst
GENICE . . . . Janelle Kester
GREEN MAN . . . . Miguel Castellano

Prior to this production, ***GREEN MAN*** underwent various readings. Director Frank Condon at The River Stage in Sacramento staged a very helpful developmental reading; John Pietrowski at Playwrights Theatre of New Jersey guided the play through readings at PTNJ and for the National New Play Network at New Jersey Rep.

GREEN MAN was originally workshopped by Premiere Stages (John Wooten, Producing Artistic Director) at Kean University in 2008 in the Murphy Dunn Theatre. The director was John Pietrowski. The cast was as follows:

ABIGAIL . . . . Edelen McWilliams
RONALD . . . . Chris Tomaino
GENICE . . . . Carolyn Stone
GREEN MAN . . . . Spiff Wiegand

Evan Cabnet directed a reading as part of the Outloud Series at Ars Nova (Renee Blinkwolt, Managing Director; Jason Eagan, Artistic Director) in New York City on April 7, 2008.

ABIGAIL . . . . Susan Pourfar
RONALD . . . . Gareth Saxe
GENICE . . . . Jennifer Mudge
GREEN MAN . . . . Ryan O'Nan

CHARACTERS

ABIGAIL – An artist

RONALD – An architect, her husband

GENICE – A stone sculptor

GREEN MAN – A man painted green. Also **GREGORY** and **GARY**

ABIGAIL, RONALD and **GENICE** are in their thirties. The characters **GREEN MAN** plays are in their twenties.

TIME

The time is roughly the present.

SETTING

In a city with tall buildings.

AUTHOR'S NOTE

The set needs to move from **ABIGAIL** and **RONALD**'s living room to **GENICE**'s living room, with stops between at **RONALD**'s implied office, a hospital space, etc. There will be a man-sized sculpture of a gargoyle that will take shape in **GENICE**'s space.

The songs "IN THE GARDEN" and "THE STARS" have all been composed by Jim Knable, copyright 2006.

STYLE NOTE

Events happening before the action of this play may be tragic, but at no point should the characters be playing high tragedy – this will undermine the play's natural development. These characters are dealing with a grief which floats, often absurd in its detachment. They are aware of themselves; they deflect emotion, even when it's boiling over, until it overcomes them and they can finally acknowledge it.

"Form ever follows function."

– Louis Sullivan

ACT ONE

Scene One

(A living room in a big city apartment. A sofa and chair. A very prominent window is stage left. **ABIGAIL JOHANSON***, 33, stands painting at an easel. Her subject is a young naked man painted entirely green, posed in the crouched attack position of a gargoyle.* **ABIGAIL** *paints in silence. More silence.)*

GREEN MAN. So. Do you have any kids?

*(***ABIGAIL*** stops.)*

ABIGAIL. Shh. Hold still.

GREEN MAN. Sorry. I've never done this. I thought I could talk.

ABIGAIL. I'd prefer that you didn't.

GREEN MAN. Okay.

(Silence. She starts painting again.)

I'm sorry. I didn't realize how long this was going to take; can I have something to put my knees on? I don't think I can hold this –

*(***ABIGAIL*** reaches behind her and grabs a stack of art books. She places them under* **GREEN MAN***'s knees, propping him up so he can hold the position.)*

Thank you. I didn't think this was going to be so hard.

ABIGAIL. If you're going to keep modeling, you better get used to it.

GREEN MAN. Can I make a confession?

ABIGAIL. If you must.

GREEN MAN. I didn't really think I was going to be modeling for you.

ABIGAIL. But you responded to the ad.

GREEN MAN. "Willing to be naked and covered with paint." I thought maybe it was something else you wanted.

ABIGAIL. Nope. Sorry. Do you want to leave?

GREEN MAN. No. It's fine. I mean, I need the money.

ABIGAIL. Can you get back in the full pose, please?

(*He does. Silence. She paints.*)

You thought I was a lonely weird housewife or something?

GREEN MAN. Well, yes.

ABIGAIL. Is that your usual gig?

GREEN MAN. No. But –

ABIGAIL. Wishful thinking.

GREEN MAN. Yeah.

ABIGAIL. You wouldn't have a problem prostituting yourself?

GREEN MAN. Is that bad?

ABIGAIL. How old are you?

GREEN MAN. Twenty. You?

(*She gives him a look.*)

Sorry.

ABIGAIL. How old do I look?

GREEN MAN. Um…

ABIGAIL. It's okay, you can say.

GREEN MAN. Definitely under forty. Thirty-eight.

ABIGAIL. (*dismally*) Thirty-three.

It's all right. It's the grey hair. I've looked this old since I was your age.

GREEN MAN. I doubt that.

(*She glares at him.*)

I mean – shit. I'll just stop talking.

ABIGAIL. Please.

(silence)

GREEN MAN. I think you're very attractive.

ABIGAIL. Shh.

GREEN MAN. I'm not just saying that. I was really excited when you opened the door and handed me the paint.

ABIGAIL. Yes, I remember.

GREEN MAN. I don't even have like an Oedipal Complex or anything. I just thought you were hot.

ABIGAIL. Thank you. I get the point.

GREEN MAN. That's a wedding ring, right?

ABIGAIL. Yes.

GREEN MAN. He's a lucky man.

ABIGAIL. Don't tell him that.

GREEN MAN. What does he do?

ABIGAIL. He's an architect.

GREEN MAN. Oh yeah? That's cool. So an artist and an architect. Did you meet in art school?

ABIGAIL. We met in Greece. We were both looking at the same ruins.

GREEN MAN. God, that's really romantic.

ABIGAIL. Yes, it was.

GREEN MAN. So can I ask you a question?

Why am I naked and painted green?

ABIGAIL. You're a gargoyle.

GREEN MAN. Oh. Like on rooftops?

ABIGAIL. Yeah, sort of.

GREEN MAN. And you really needed me painted green for this?

ABIGAIL. *Yes.*

(calmer)

I wanted to see what this light would do off green skin.

GREEN MAN. Why gargoyles?

ABIGAIL. Just because.

GREEN MAN. You're just into them?

ABIGAIL. Yeah.

GREEN MAN. Do you want me to do something with my face?

ABIGAIL. Excuse me?

GREEN MAN. If I'm a gargoyle, shouldn't I be snarling or gnashing my teeth or whatever?

ABIGAIL. I'll handle that part. I won't ask you to make faces.

GREEN MAN. I could do it. Watch.

(He makes a hideous face, first at a profile to her, then he turns to her. She drops her paintbrush and steps back, truly scared suddenly. He drops the face.)

Oh shit, sorry. I didn't mean to. I was just being funny. What did I do?

ABIGAIL. Nothing. Just don't do it again.

Look. Forget it, forget this. This was a bad idea. Put your clothes on. You can wash the paint off in the shower. This is bad for me.

(She takes the canvas and puts it down, folds up the easel.)

Go on, please. We're done. I'll write you a check for the full amount. Thank you for coming.

GREEN MAN. Aw, Abigail, you don't have to do that. I'll stop goofing around. I'll do it right. You don't have to –

ABIGAIL. Yes, I do. Please.

(hearing something)

Oh Christ.

GREEN MAN. What.

ABIGAIL. The elevator. My husband's coming up. He can't see you. He can't see this. Hide. I'll pay you double. Go lie down in the bathtub, pull the shower curtain, don't make any noise. Please, I beg you.

GREEN MAN. But we didn't –

ABIGAIL. *I beg you.*

(He looks at her. He goes off to the bathroom. She quickly does her best to get rid of all evidence of his existence. The front door opens. **RONALD JOHANSON**, *35, enters.)*

RONALD. Hi. I forgot my files for the presentation. Can you believe that? Like my head wasn't screwed on. Hi, baby.

(He kisses her.)

Are you okay?

ABIGAIL. Yeah.

RONALD. Were you painting?

ABIGAIL. A while ago.

RONALD. Do I get to see anything?

ABIGAIL. Soon.

(He heads off for the bedroom, talking when he's on and off.)

RONALD. This thing is driving me nuts! What do they expect me to do? You know?

ABIGAIL. The Newton Building?

RONALD. Yeah, what else? Are there going to be buildings *next* to it or aren't there? It's a simple question that should have a simple answer. I am an architect. I need some context. And this is a simple concept, right?

(He's out in the living room now, holding his files.)

ABIGAIL. Very.

RONALD. But it's like I'm speaking… Aramaic or something. Martian. "Why can't you just make the building so it works either way?" So I go: "If a friend comes over for dinner, don't you want to know if he's in Alcoholics Anonymous first before you offer him a drink?"

*(**ABIGAIL** looks at him with some question.)*

All right, so it wasn't the best comparison. I was trying everything.

How's your day been so far?

ABIGAIL. Fine. I told you.

RONALD. You look a little pale.

ABIGAIL. I haven't gone running yet. Too much coffee.

RONALD. That sculptor's supposed to come over tonight. For dinner. Is that still okay?

ABIGAIL. Yes. I was counting on it.

RONALD. You'll like her. Her stuff's very gothic. You'll love it. Now if I can just get someone to tell me how many sides of the damn building are going to be exposed, we'll be in business!

All right, back to work. I love you. I'll call you before I leave.

(He kisses her. They separate and look at each other for a second, sharing something very sad and unspoken. He exits out the front door. Silence. **GREEN MAN** *comes out of the bathroom.)*

GREEN MAN. Good thing he didn't have to take a piss, huh?

(The front door flies open again and **RONALD** *enters, completely unaware of* **GREEN MAN.** *)*

RONALD. I forgot, I really had to take a leak.

GREEN MAN. I didn't touch her! She was painting me! I didn't do anything. I'm sorry!

*(***GREEN MAN*** runs to the window and leaps out into the implied void.* **ABIGAIL** *screams.* **RONALD** *steps intently to the window and closes it. He goes to* **ABIGAIL** *and holds her to him.)*

RONALD. It's okay, It's okay, I'm right here. Why was the window open?

ABIGAIL. I needed some air.

RONALD. Why did you scream?

ABIGAIL. You scared me, bursting back in like that.

RONALD. Did you take your pills?

ABIGAIL. Yes. No. I was waiting.

(She's silent. **RONALD** *turns from her, goes to the bathroom, comes back with a pill bottle. She takes the pill bottle from his hand, opens it and takes one quickly.)*

RONALD. I'll call in and tell them to go on without me.

ABIGAIL. No, don't.

RONALD. I can't leave you like this.

ABIGAIL. But you always do.

RONALD. Stop it.

ABIGAIL. I'll be okay. The pills'll kick in.

RONALD. Come here.

(*She pulls away from him.*)

ABIGAIL. I want you to go. I want to be alone.

RONALD. Abby…

ABIGAIL. Please. Go back to work. I'll be okay. You need to be at work or they'll end up bulldozing you into something you don't want later. Go on.

(*He looks at her. There's not much she's going to let him do beyond what she's asked.*)

RONALD. Are you going to be all right?

ABIGAIL. Yeah. I won't paint anything, but I'll be fine.

RONALD. I'll cancel this dinner tonight.

ABIGAIL. No. Don't.

RONALD. Are you sure?

ABIGAIL. Yes.

RONALD. I love you more than anything.

ABIGAIL. I love you, too. Go back to work. I'm fine. Call me later. Go.

(*She opens the front door for him.*)

RONALD. You call me if –

ABIGAIL. I will.

(*He kisses her and exits. She closes the door behind him. Silence. She picks up her canvas. The bathroom door opens.* **GREEN MAN** *comes out as before, now without emotion, grabs the canvas from* **ABIGAIL**'s *hand, goes to the window, opens it and jumps out with the painting. This time* **ABIGAIL** *just watches blankly.*)

Scene Two

(Lights pop up on **RONALD**, **ABIGAIL** *and* **GENICE** *mid-conversation on the sofa and chair.)*

GENICE. So there's a dragon that terrorizes this French town called Rouen. He comes every year demanding a virgin, sometimes he gets one, sometimes they're all out and they have to give him a soldier. They hate the dragon, obviously, but they live in fear of being destroyed, so they always comply. Then one day a Priest comes along – and this is in the twelfth century so not everybody in Europe was Christian. So this village was a bunch of pagans. Where was I?

ABIGAIL. Priest.

GENICE. Yes. He says to them, I will get rid of your dragon problem if you will build and join my church. And they say –

RONALD. "Yeah, right."

GENICE. No. They say, okay. And he goes up to Dragon Mountain and easily subdues the dragon with the sign of the cross and holy water and Christianity and leads him down into town on a leash. He is peaceful now, completely subdued by the priest. Harmless. But the townspeople don't want to take any chances so they burn him at the stake.

ABIGAIL. The priest?

GENICE. The dragon. However, his head and neck are so hard from breathing fire all the time that those parts don't burn. So the people build the church and join it, and they mount the head and neck of the dragon on top of the church as a reminder of Christian victory over evil and oppression.

ABIGAIL. That's a good story.

GENICE. There are lots of stories. Of course, by strict definition – which, by the way, is my definition – it is only actually a gargoyle if it serves the practical purpose.

RONALD. And the practical purpose is…

GENICE. A water spout to keep the rain off the sides and base of the building. Fashioned into an animal or a demon, perhaps, but the water must collect in it from the roof then shoot out of the mouth or any other orifice. Gargoyle, Garg, the Latin for throat, that's where it comes from. You have them on this building. Some of my favorite in the city. You are very lucky.

ABIGAIL. What if it doesn't serve the practical purpose?

GENICE. Then it's just a grotesque. Which could be anything from a statue to a face carved in a wall. Funny you should mention because I'm interested in how grotesques and gargoyles can intersect. Especially in the English tradition…

RONALD. Are you sure you don't want a drink, Genice? I'm going to get one for myself.

GENICE. No thank you, I'm a recovering alcoholic.

(**ABIGAIL** *stifles a laugh, turns it into a cough.*)

RONALD. Oh God. I'm sorry.

GENICE. You go ahead, though. I don't mind. In fact, I enjoy watching a little. Go on.

RONALD. Thanks. Abby?

ABIGAIL. Jim Beam and Coke.

(**RONALD** *gets up and goes to get drinks elsewhere in the room.*)

GENICE. Abby, I understand you're a very talented painter.

ABIGAIL. You probably heard that from my husband.

GENICE. No, actually, I have a colleague who knows your work. I mentioned I was coming for dinner and she said I should ask what you were up to lately.

ABIGAIL. That's very kind.

GENICE. Joyce Bonnefield.

ABIGAIL. Sounds familiar.

GENICE. So what are you up to lately?

(**RONALD** *swings by with the drinks, giving* **ABIGAIL** *hers.*)

RONALD. I'm sorry, Genice, I should have asked you if you wanted a soda or water. We have juice.

GENICE. Water's fine, thank you.

ABIGAIL. Thank you, Ronald.

RONALD. The food is almost ready, also.

GENICE. You're right, that's a terrible question. It's just something we get used to asking each other, right? I hate when people ask what I'm up to, because half the time it's nothing. I went through a very long period when I couldn't work at all and all anyone asked was what I was up to. And I just wanted to say: Absolutely nothing, I'm an utter failure, are you happy? Not that you're a failure. I'm not saying it right. I understand you, that's all.

ABIGAIL. What got you going again?

GENICE. Excuse me?

ABIGAIL. What got you to start working again?

GENICE. Gargoyles. Actually, yes, gargoyles. I hadn't worked on anything for…years, actually. Then one day I was walking downtown and I looked up and saw one. His eyes were sunken and his cheek bones and chin were sharp and hard. His hands and feet were like claws, his chest puffed out like a bird's. He was so powerful and still. It just captured my imagination. I wanted to make one. So I tried it. And I found that that I loved it. Because it was more than art. It was…useful.

ABIGAIL. Are you saying art is not useful?

GENICE. No, no, of course not. I just mean there's physical, practical, unarguable value in it.

ABIGAIL. It's lucky you saw a gargoyle and not a parking garage.

RONALD. Maybe we should sit down and eat.

GENICE. Listen. I know about what happened.

(*pause*)

Forgive me. I just wanted to say it and get it out there. Joyce told me.

I'm very sorry that…it's terrible. I feel terrible for both of you.

(**RONALD** *and* **ABIGAIL** *just look at her.*)

Should I go?

ABIGAIL.	RONALD.
Yes.	No.

RONALD. Abby…

(**ABIGAIL** *looks away, right at* **GREEN MAN**, *who is now perched in the open window. She goes quickly to the window, the* **GREEN MAN** *jumps out and off, she shuts the window.*)

GENICE. I'll go.

(She gets up.)

RONALD. No. Stay. Please.

GENICE. It isn't my business. I just had to say something because it was like a, you know, pink elephant. Like try not to think about a pink elephant.

ABIGAIL. *(going to the kitchen area)* And don't offer a drink to an alcoholic.

RONALD. Come on…

GENICE. Right. Exactly. We all have things we don't talk about directly. That's why I don't drink anymore, actually. All I did was say things I shouldn't. Hurt people. It's amazing how you can hurt people just by telling the truth.

But dinner smells wonderful.

RONALD. It's Abigail's specialty.

GENICE. It smells delicious, Abigail.

ABIGAIL. Thanks.

GENICE. I won't be offended if you want me to leave. Truly.

ABIGAIL. No. Let's eat.

Scene Three

(GENICE's *apartment. Later.* GENICE *enters, a little tipsy. She flops on the sofa and takes off her shoes.*)

GENICE. Are you awake?

I'm sorry I'm so late. They're very nice, you'll like them. I only made one social faux pax and that was inevitable.

Are you even awake or am I just talking to myself?

(GREGORY, *same actor as* GREEN MAN, *still green, enters.*)

GREGORY. Both. Start again. Why are you so late?

GENICE. I had a drink. Or two.

GREGORY. Oh for Christsakes…

GENICE. I'm sorry.

GREGORY. I knew I should've gone with you.

GENICE. You can't go with me all the time. I have to be able to do it on my own. That's the problem…when I'm on my own. That's when I'm weak. I'm sorry, Gregory.

GREGORY. I can smell you from here.

GENICE. I didn't have that much.

GREGORY. You smell like a bar.

GENICE. I brushed my teeth. I had a mint.

GREGORY. You're hopeless.

GENICE. You love me anyway, don't you.

GREGORY. Of course. That's my curse. You're my addiction.

(*lays his head in her lap*)

It was your idea, you said you had the problem.

GENICE. You said I had the problem. I realized you were right.

GREGORY. What am I going to do with you?

GENICE. Throw me out a window.

Oh God.

(beat)

I told them I knew about what happened. They didn't want to talk about it.

They have their own way. Everyone has their own way, I guess. I shouldn't have said anything, I meant to let them bring it up if it came up. But how could it not come up?

GREGORY. Did you say it before or after drinking?

GENICE. Before, thank you very much. And then we ate and talked more about gargoyles and before I knew it I had a drink in my hand.

GREGORY. Just like that?

GENICE. They had glasses out. They had bottles out. It just happened. I guess they figured they had their thing and I had mine and we would just know what we knew and go on doing what made us comfortable.

Would you play me something?

GREGORY. You don't deserve it.

GENICE. Come on, please?

GREGORY. You don't deserve it.

(He gets up and goes off to the bedroom.)

GENICE. Gregory. Stop it. You're no better. When you quit smoking. Every time you quit smoking and you'd come home. I could smell you, too. That stinks worse. I could smell it in your hair.

Gregory?

(Pause. He walks out of the bedroom with a guitar slung over his shoulder. He plays for her.)

(Music: "In the Garden")

SIGHT UNSEEN
I WILL TAKE IT ALL
HOUSE AND KEYS
AND THE GARDEN
IT'S A PERFECT THEME

FOR A NIGHT IN FALL
ALL THE LEAVES
ARE FALLIN'

YOU AND ME
AND THE CASTLE WALLS
QUIETLY, TELLING OUR LIVES
THERE'S SO MANY THINGS
YOU'LL NEVER KNOW
ABOUT ME
THAT I HIDE

HOW LIKE THE WIND TO PLAY TRICKS WITH THE SOUNDS
    OF THE NIGHT
IN THE GARDEN
YOU WERE RIGHT
I WAS ONLY STARTING
STAY WITH ME
I WILL TELL IT ALL
PATIENTLY
WHILE YOU AWAIT
IT'S THE HARDEST THING
TO OPEN
YOURSELF UP TO TAKE

HOW LIKE THE WIND TO PLAY TRICKS WITH THE SOUNDS
    OF THE NIGHT
IN THE GARDEN
YOU WERE RIGHT
I WAS ONLY STARTING

(Her eyes are closed by now. He walks away with the guitar. Silence. She opens her eyes. Looks around.)

Gregory?

(Lights shift.)

Scene Four

(**RONALD** *at work, at a drafting table. He speaks on a phone.*)

RONALD. Big stone monsters with wings and claws and fangs. Because they're classy. Yes, I think it's a wonderful idea. She's good, she'll do a good job. Because she comes highly recommended and I've seen her portfolio. Well, you can trust me or look at it yourself, but it's already been approved, so if you want to derail it, you'd better be quick. No, nothing's wrong. I've been under a lot of stress. I know. You are a friend. Thank you. Look, I've got to go. I'll have it sent to you right away. I know. You're just doing your job. Bye.

(*He hangs up.*)

And I'm just trying to do mine, you prissy little motherfucker.

(*He throws his pencil down, breathes for a second. He's trying to hold it together. His phone rings.*)

What!

(**ABIGAIL** *appears.*)

ABIGAIL. Nice greeting.

RONALD. Abby, shit, sorry Abby. I thought you were… I'm sorry, honey. Neil's being a little shit. What's up?

ABIGAIL. You wanted to have lunch. I was waiting for you. It's three o'clock.

RONALD. Oh fuck.

ABIGAIL. Forget it.

RONALD. Are you okay?

ABIGAIL. Yeah. Hungry, but I'll just make something for myself now.

RONALD. I'm sorry, honey. Everything's going wrong today. Every time I get excited about something some bureaucratic prick sweeps the rug out from under me. Neil's gonna nix Genice, I'm sure of it.

ABIGAIL. How do you know?

RONALD. It's too hokey for him, too old fashioned or some
bullshit. And he has Grady's ear when it comes to
anything style-related because that's why Grady hired
him, 'cause he's a prissy little…

ABIGAIL. Don't you have to be careful about the way you
talk about people at your office.

RONALD. Nobody's here. Everyone's off at lunch.

ABIGAIL. It'll be okay.

RONALD. Maybe.

ABIGAIL. Go take a walk. I took a walk this morning.

RONALD. Did you? To the park?

ABIGAIL. Yeah.

RONALD. Past the carousel?

ABIGAIL. Yeah.

(Silence.)

RONALD. I cried in the men's room this morning. I just
broke down sobbing.

(Silence.)

ABIGAIL. Call me before you come home.

RONALD. All right. I love you.

ABIGAIL. Love you.

*(She hangs up and exits. He hangs up. Looks down at
his drafting table. Beat. Picks up his pencil, thinking of
what to do next.* **GARY** *[***GREEN MAN***] appears in a nice
dress shirt and slacks, still green underneath.)*

GARY. Excuse me. Mr. Johanson.

*(***RONALD** *turns to him.)*

Hi. I'm your intern. Gary. Sorry to just show up. The
secretary wasn't there so I just…

RONALD. Gary, yes. I remember. Nice to meet you. I forgot
you were coming today. Please, come in.

GARY. It looks like you're working, I don't want to interrupt
you.

RONALD. I was on a break. I haven't had lunch yet, have you?

GARY. Yeah.

RONALD. Well, come with me anyway. I'll buy you a coffee.

(**RONALD** *is walking* **GARY** *offstage.*)

So what college are you from again?

(*They're off.* **GENICE** *has moved on. She stands above a large block of solid rock – probably something that's been onstage the whole time. This piece will change over the course of the play as* **GENICE** *sculpts it…so it probably isn't actually made of solid rock. She holds a hammer and a chisel. She moves around the rock, sizing it up, deciding where to start.*)

GENICE. (*to the rock*) Where are you? I see you in there.

(*She gives the chisel a whack. A sound more akin to a hammer hitting a railroad stake rings out. Lights move to* **RONALD** *and* **GARY** *on a bench.* **RONALD** *eats a sandwich,* **GARY** *drinks a coffee.*)

RONALD. So why do you want to be an architect?

GARY. Louis Sullivan.

RONALD. Really?

GARY. I didn't even know who he was until last year. His buildings are so…monumental. They're like mountains. I've never been so inspired by something. It's like I know how to look at the world now.

RONALD. I remember that feeling. It was Sullivan for me, too.

GARY. I can tell how you're influenced by him.

RONALD. You mean how I shamelessly plagiarize his ideas.

GARY. No, I didn't mean that.

RONALD. It's okay. I'm proud. He's papa Louis. He gives a little to everybody.

This thing I'm working on now… I think about him a lot. Because of the ornamentation.

GARY. I love his ornamentation.

RONALD. I figured you would.

GARY. Is it the building you were talking about on the phone? The Newton...

RONALD. The very one.

But I tell you, Gary, there's the difference between Louis and me. He could get what he wanted done. Nowadays... I barely even know what I'm building anymore.

GARY. You don't really mean that.

(**RONALD** *looks at him. He does.*)

RONALD. How old are you? Twenty, twenty-one?

GARY. Just turned.

RONALD. I remember being twenty-one. That was an exciting time. Did you go and get really drunk for your birthday?

GARY. Of course.

RONALD. What'd you go to a sleazy bar or something?

GARY. Strip club.

RONALD. Well, all right, that's more like it! You and your buddies.

GARY. Yeah.

RONALD. I hope you remembered it the next day.

GARY. Most of it.

(**RONALD** *laughs.*)

RONALD. I did that once. Back in my single days.

GARY. How long have you been married?

RONALD. Married, four years. Together with her, six.

GARY. That's nice.

RONALD. Yes. It's very nice.

So did you get a lap dance?

GARY. Of course not, those are illegal.

RONALD. Liar.

Do you have a girlfriend?

GARY. Not right now. I did. We broke up.

RONALD. Not because of the strip club.

GARY. No.

RONALD. Was it like a big thing? The relationship.

GARY. Yeah, kind of. I guess not. She's already on to the next guy.

RONALD. Ah, college. A time of many conquests of little consequence.

You know, I've never cheated on my wife.

GARY. Oh?

RONALD. Sorry, didn't mean to lay that one on ya.

But it's a respectable thing, right? Things happen, opportunities present themselves and you have to choose. Love is a choice, sometimes. Sometimes you don't even feel so in love with the person at the time, but you still choose them over the fleeting romance because you know she's the one who counts in the end. When you find someone who you can be with like that…to risk losing them is to risk losing the best parts of yourself.

But you can't help remembering your stupid young and carefree days with a little bit of longing.

Listen to me, I remember my uncle talking to me like this. My older brothers. My father. Some crazy old man in a bar. I'm becoming all of them. I'm getting old.

GARY. Why did you want to become an architect?

RONALD. I don't know, to get chicks.

(He laughs.)

No. Because it called to me or something. Like you said. It moved me, the idea of making buildings where people would live and work. Creating the designs of structures that fill cities. Such a basic thing. I have to remind myself of that sometimes, where the passion came from. There's a lot of other stuff you have to deal with. There always is. Now I definitely sound like my father.

God, I'm depressing. Are you sure you want to intern for me?

GARY. Yes.

RONALD. Why?

GARY. I think you're a really great architect.

*(**RONALD** smiles.)*

RONALD. All right. You're hired.

*(Lights go to **GENICE**, leaving them. The rock has gone through chipping. Nothing much can be made out form-wise, but the shape is changing.)*

GENICE. Play something on the piano for me, would you? Something heavy. I need some inspiration.

*(The piano starts up. Grave from Beethoven's Pathetique Piano Sonata. **GENICE** circles the rock. She's barefoot now. She works to the music. Once her mode of reinvigorated toiling is set, lights rise also on **RONALD** and **ABIGAIL**'s living space. **RONALD** is coming home. He and **ABIGAIL** kiss and immediately go about bringing food and wine out for dinner. They set their places and start eating. All without talking. Like a ritual. Music gets softer but plays underneath **GENICE**'s speech. She is talking while working…talking like she works, with intention.)*

You are medieval. From the dark ages. In the shadows lit by candle flames. When no one could read and images told stories. And we are the stone cutters who make the images last. On the castle walls. Under a thousand years of rain.

*(Music stops. **GREGORY** has entered, watching her work.)*

GREGORY. You're making another gargoyle.

GENICE. Yes. But it's more this time.

GREGORY. Looks like a gargoyle.

GENICE. And it'll work like a gargoyle. But it won't have a gargoyle's face. It'll have the face of a Green Man.

GREGORY. Explain.

GENICE. The Irish Green Man. It's a kind of grotesque, just a round happy generous face on a wall. He's the spirit of the woods, the mysterious and deep woods of birth, death and rejuvenation. The Green Man is good. Different from a gargoyle. Gargoyles are the demons you want up on the roof. The Green Man is never a gargoyle. But this will be a Green Man who is. Something new, something ancient. A beautiful hideous beast who calls the rain down, who summons it to fall all over his tortured body then pours it on the ground where it will sprout trees.

GREGORY. I love watching you work. Hearing the hammer on the chisel. The way your face gets hard like your own statue, the moves you make circling your creation. Finding it in the rock. It's very sexy.

GENICE. What do you think of my idea? About the Green Man Gargoyle.

GREGORY. I think it's a fine idea. I'm not sure anyone will go for it.

GENICE. Why not?

GREGORY. People don't like to think that something beautiful can come from something ugly.

GENICE. I think the opposite is true, darling. I think that's what people hope for.

(Lights fall on them.)

ABIGAIL. How was the rest of your day?

RONALD. Good.

ABIGAIL. Really? You sounded awful when I talked to you.

RONALD. I went outside, like you suggested.

ABIGAIL. Took a walk?

RONALD. Had lunch.

ABIGAIL. By yourself?

(pause)

RONALD. No.

There's this kid who's going to start working with me. An intern. Bright-eyed, bushy-tailed.

ABIGAIL. You had lunch with him?

RONALD. Yes.

ABIGAIL. Well. That's nice.

RONALD. You're not mad, are you?

ABIGAIL. No. You could have called and told me that was your plan. I waited for you here.

RONALD. It wasn't planned. It just happened.

ABIGAIL. It's fine, I don't care.

RONALD. You're not seriously angry, are you?

ABIGAIL. Is it really a him?

RONALD. What?

ABIGAIL. You're sure it's not a twenty-year-old co-ed with blonde hair and perky breasts?

RONALD. I'm not even going to respond to that.

ABIGAIL. Pleading the fifth, huh?

(She gets up to clear the dishes.)

RONALD. You're being ridiculous. He's a guy. He's my intern. We bonded over talking about carefree college guy stuff.

ABIGAIL. Carefree college guy stuff?

RONALD. There's just no way I'm going to win this, is there? You want a fight.

ABIGAIL. And you want to be in college again, apparently.

RONALD. Give me those.

(He takes the dishes and storms off.)

ABIGAIL. The rest of my day was good, too. A strapping young man came over and posed nude for me.

RONALD. *(off)* How nice for you!

ABIGAIL. At least he got aroused when he saw me.

(RONALD *enters, staring at her angrily, still holding a plate.*)

RONALD. That's not fair.

ABIGAIL. Don't worry, I told him I was married. Not that that would have stopped him…

RONALD. Did you also tell him you were delusional lunatic?

(*silence*)

ABIGAIL. Now *that* is not fair.

(*silence*)

RONALD. You're right. I'm sorry.

I don't really think –

ABIGAIL. Yes, you do. And it's true. Your wife's flown the coop.

Here, I'll go take one of my happy pills and get normal for you.

RONALD. Abby…

ABIGAIL. What!

RONALD. You're not a lunatic. I'm sorry.

Look, can we just call a truce? Can we stop fighting for the sake of talking?

I'm tired.

ABIGAIL. Well, roll over and go to sleep. You always do.

(RONALD *smashes the plate he's holding to the floor, where it shatters. They stare at each other, both a little scared. He exits. She gets up and picks up the plate pieces. He comes in again, sees her, goes to help her. They get it cleaned up.*)

RONALD. I didn't mean to do that.

ABIGAIL. I know. I didn't mean to say that.

(*They stand together. Silence.*)

RONALD. Do you still want to go to this thing tonight?

ABIGAIL. What thing?

RONALD. The Party.

ABIGAIL. You never told me about it.

RONALD. I know I told you about it.

ABIGAIL. You go on.

RONALD. I think it might be good for you to go. Good for us. We can dress up. Get out of this place.

Please.

(pause)

ABIGAIL. All right.

Scene Five

(Lights shift to The **GREEN MAN**, *dressed in a tuxedo, sitting at a keyboard, playing a spicy Latin version of "In the Garden" – party music. Sounds of voices talking festively.* **GENICE** *enters, holding a champagne flute. She watches the* **GREEN MAN** *play. He becomes* **GREGORY** *to her.)*

GENICE. Thank you for agreeing to do this.

GREGORY. Anything for the cause. And the paycheck. You look lovely.

GENICE. Thank you. You look pretty cute in your penguin suit.

GREGORY. Go on, go talk to people, promote yourself.

GENICE. I'll try to find Ronald. I really want you to meet him. He's a good man.

GREGORY. Go find him.

GENICE. I love you.

(She kisses the top of his head while he plays and walks off. **RONALD** *enters alone, wearing a rumpled sports jacket, carrying a drink. He walks up to the* **GREEN MAN.** *He becomes* **GARY** *to him.)*

RONALD. Well I'll be damned. I thought the piano player looked familiar.

*(***GARY*** stops playing.)*

GARY. I couldn't resist. Lessons since seven.

RONALD. You sound great. A man of many talents. What do you think of this party? Hardly a raging kegger, huh?

GARY. Well…

RONALD. I never feel comfortable at these things. Always feeling I'm supposed to say something significant about my work or *the* work or everyone else's work. Here, have a drink.

GARY. That's your drink.

RONALD. I haven't touched it yet. I'll get another one.

GARY. Is that your wife over there?

RONALD. Yes.

GARY. She's pretty. Pretty and sad.

RONALD. I shouldn't leave her alone too long. She used to be so good at these parties. She was always the social one. I was the social imbecile. She could talk to anyone about anything, make them feel good. Now she can barely function in public.

GARY. Barely function? How come?

RONALD. Something happened.

GARY. To her?

RONALD. To us.

I'd love for her to meet you. Don't go anywhere. And don't stop playing.

(**GREEN MAN** *plays lighter and lighter, then stops and slips off.* **RONALD** *starts to exit, but runs into* **GENICE.**)

GENICE. Oh, hi, I was looking for you.

RONALD. You were?

GENICE. I don't know anyone else here. Slightly different crowd than I'm used to.

RONALD. You look lovely.

GENICE. So do you. Is Abigail here?

RONALD. Over by the punch bowl.

GENICE. I started a gargoyle.

RONALD. Oh yeah? That's great.

GENICE. I'm still on the project, aren't I?

RONALD. Yes, of course. Why?

GENICE. Something in your voice.

RONALD. It's just there's some red tape to cut through. A couple jerks to overcome. It'll work itself out. What sort of gargoyle is it? I'd love to see it. If you let people see your stuff in progress.

GENICE. Sure, just come over sometime. It's an idea I'm really excited about. It's a Green Man.

RONALD. *(jarred)* A…green man?

GENICE. You're not familiar? It's an Irish thing. It's a myth. The Green Man is the benevolent spirit of the woods.

(They walk off talking. **ABIGAIL** *enters with a drink on a different part of the stage.* **GREEN MAN** *walks up to her as a caterer, with a tray of food.)*

GREEN MAN. Cocktail weenie?

ABIGAIL. No thanks – You!

GREEN MAN. Oh my God. You.

ABIGAIL. What are you doing here?

GREEN MAN. Catering. Yourself?

ABIGAIL. My husband.

GREEN MAN. Oh right, of course. The architect.

Hey, how did you…explain things to him?

ABIGAIL. I let him think I imagined you.

GREEN MAN. And that worked?

ABIGAIL. That's the advantage of cracking up: people are very willing to believe you're crazy.

GREEN MAN. How's the painting going?

ABIGAIL. Uninspired.

GREEN MAN. You want me to come over some time?

To pose for you again.

ABIGAIL. Yes. Yes, I'd like that.

How did you survive, anyway? The fall. I was sure you were gone.

GREEN MAN. A statue below your window caught me. In its outstretched arms.

ABIGAIL. A gargoyle.

GREEN MAN. Yes, as a matter of fact. Funny coincidence, huh?

RONALD. *(from off)* Abigail!

(He enters with **GENICE.** *)*

Look who I found.

*(**GREEN MAN** has slipped offstage.)*

GENICE. Hi, Abby.

ABIGAIL. Hi.

GENICE. I was just telling your husband how happy I am to find you both here. Everyone else makes me nervous.

ABIGAIL. You're drinking.

GENICE. Yeah. But it's mainly just a prop. I've been working on the same one since I came.

ABIGAIL. Is that intern here, Ronald?

RONALD. Huh? Oh. Yeah. He's here. I just saw him. He was playing piano.

GENICE. The man playing piano is your intern?

RONALD. Well, no not exactly. My intern sat in for a second while the real piano player took a break. He's full of surprises.

GENICE. *(just falling out of her mouth)* My fiancé was a musician.

(Silence. They both look at her.)

ABIGAIL. You never mentioned you had a fiancé.

GENICE. Former. Oh, look, I did finish it after all. More for anyone else?

*(**RONALD** shakes his head. **ABIGAIL** hands her her glass.)*

I'll be right back.

(She exits.)

ABIGAIL. I guess it was a hard break-up.

RONALD. What?

ABIGAIL. With her former fiancé. Suddenly I like her more.

What's he look like?

RONALD. Her fiancé?

ABIGAIL. Your intern.

RONALD. You know, like your average guy. Medium height, build, hair.

*(***GREEN MAN*** has slipped on again and is playing the
piano.)*

ABIGAIL. *(motioning to* **GREEN MAN***)* Is that him?

(beat)

RONALD. No. That's the real piano player.

(Pause. They listen to him.)

Do you want to go soon?

ABIGAIL. He has such a delicate touch. Such sweet little
hands.

*(***RONALD*** puts his hand on her shoulder. They listen.
She puts her hand on his hand, takes it off her shoulder
but still holds it, looks at it carefully.)*

Your hands are so big. Like a lumberjack's hands. Your
hands were made for swinging axes.

Why don't we invite Genice to come back to our place?

RONALD. But I thought you –

ABIGAIL. I told you, I like her now.

(She walks away. **GREEN MAN** *looks up at* **RONALD***.*
RONALD *turns away and walks off after his wife. Fade
to black.)*

Scene Six

*(Lights up on **RONALD**, **ABIGAIL** and **GENICE** playing
Twister. **RONALD** and **GENICE** are on the mat with all
those crazy colored circles. **ABIGAIL** is on the sidelines,
spinning the pointer.)*

ABIGAIL. Right hand red.

*(**RONALD** and **GENICE** put their right hands on Red
circles. They are pretty drunk by this point, so this is not
as easy as it should be.)*

Left foot green.

*(They comply. Their bodies are in a contortion that could
be misread as vaguely sexual.)*

Right foot blue.

Jesus, this could go on forever. Who invented this
ridiculous game?

GENICE. Why don't you join us?

ABIGAIL. Someone's got to spin the spinner.

GENICE. We'll play so that you just take turns saying hands
or feet and a color.

RONALD. Come on, Abby, don't make me do this alone.

ABIGAIL. Looks like you're doing just fine by yourself,
honey.

GENICE. I'm slipping. Give us another one at least, I can't
hold this.

ABIGAIL. Pretend it's yoga. I'm getting another drink.

*(**ABIGAIL** stands up and walks to where the drinks live.
GENICE falls, knocking **RONALD** over. They lie next to
each other, spent.)*

RONALD. I've been much more aware of how old I am
lately. I can't drink as much as I used to, that's for sure.

GENICE. That's funny, I drink more and more and it
doesn't seem to do anything.

RONALD. You just fell over.

GENICE. That had nothing to do with drinking.

(ABIGAIL *enters.*)

ABIGAIL. I always hated this game.

GENICE. Why do you own it?

RONALD. It was a gift.

ABIGAIL. His mother gave it to us. For birthday parties.

(*Pause.*)

GENICE. How old was he?

(*Silence.*)

RONALD. Two and a half.

ABIGAIL. What was your fiancé's name?

GENICE. Gregory.

ABIGAIL. Tell us about him.

(*She sits.*)

GENICE. I met him at a wedding. He was the piano player. First at the ceremony, then at the reception. Musicians are always their sexiest when they're playing. I watched him playing all day; I couldn't keep my eyes off him. He'd do this funny thing with his right foot when he was improvising. It was like it found a life of its own. Like a fish on a dock, flapping around…

ABIGAIL. Sexy.

GENICE. Worked on me. All that energy – wild, uncontrollable, uninhibited. I could picture the bed frame shaking. Do you know what I mean?

ABIGAIL. Ronald moves his ass like that when he's at the drafting table.

RONALD. I what?

ABIGAIL. Shake your ass. Your hips. You move around.

RONALD. I won't say what you do when your painting.

GENICE. Why not? Say it, say it!

RONALD. With the back of her brush, on her lips…

GENICE. Oooh.

ABIGAIL. What happened to him?

(*Beat.* **GENICE** *adjusts.*)

GENICE. What do you mean?

ABIGAIL. If he's not your fiancé anymore…

(**GENICE** *drinks.*)

GENICE. We're still together. Is that what you meant?

ABIGAIL. Yes, I suppose. Well, no, not exactly.

GENICE. We're not married. We decided in the end not to get married. It didn't suit us. Our style. But, yes we're together. He's waiting for me at home right now.

ABIGAIL. Why didn't he come to the party?

GENICE. He did.

(*They look at her.*)

He was the piano player. Funny coincidence, huh? It just happened to work out that way.

ABIGAIL. The piano player?

GENICE. I didn't say anything about him because he feels awkward being introduced when he's working. I asked him if he wanted to come with us after the party, but he'd had a long day; he wanted to go home. He's waiting for me there.

ABIGAIL. He was pretty popular, that piano player.

GENICE. Gregory's good. You see what I mean? How could I resist.

Maybe it is time I left. Thank you so much for this. It was fun.

RONALD. Anytime. We're glad to have you.

ABIGAIL. Are you going to be all right getting home? Ronald, why don't you give her a ride.

GENICE. That's okay. I can get a cab. I don't want to put you out.

RONALD. No, that's ridiculous. Let me drive you. Just gotta get my shoes on.

(*He gets up and heads off for his shoes.*)

ABIGAIL. How long have the two of you been together? You and Gregory.

GENICE. Pretty long.

ABIGAIL. When did you meet?

GENICE. College.

ABIGAIL. I've always wondered what it would have been like to meet Ronald at that age. It makes such a difference, when you meet someone in your life. We probably would have hated each other. Or hurt each other terribly. In some ways it feels like that's where we're at now. Like we've gone back in time to before we even met.

*(**RONALD** enters.)*

RONALD. Ready?

GENICE. Can I use your bathroom?

*(**RONALD** gestures back to it.)*

Thank you.

*(**GENICE** exits.)*

RONALD. Do you really feel like that?

ABIGAIL. *(about the Twister mat)* Help me fold this up.

RONALD. Abby…

ABIGAIL. Sometimes.

(She picks up the mat. He helps her fold it and put the game away.)

RONALD. I've been thinking. We should get away somewhere. The two of us. Find an island. Climb volcanoes, roll around on the beach, swim out in the ocean.

ABIGAIL. Sure, that sounds nice.

RONALD. Don't you think it would do us good?

ABIGAIL. We'd still have come back here at the end of the day.

I think Gregory left her a long time ago.

RONALD. What?

ABIGAIL. I don't think there's anyone waiting for her at home. I think she's alone.

RONALD. But why would she…

ABIGAIL. Go inside with her, at her apartment. Ask to see the gargoyle. See what she says or does. Look for evidence that he's there. I bet you won't find any.

RONALD. Why do you say that?

ABIGAIL. Because she made up the thing about the piano player. He didn't know her. He didn't know you either. You both make things up. And I'm the one who's medicated.

*(***GENICE*** enters.)*

GENICE. Ready.

Scene Seven

(RONALD and GENICE are standing outside GENICE's implied front door.)

GENICE. Thanks for the ride.

RONALD. No problem. Listen, I hope you don't have the impression that Abigail doesn't like you. She can be hot and cold. She really wanted you to come over.

GENICE. Why would I think she doesn't like me?

RONALD. She can get…aggressive.

GENICE. I didn't find her aggressive. You two have been through a lot. You're still going through it. I think you're both wonderful.

RONALD. Likewise.

Hey, do you think I could see the gargoyle?

GENICE. Now?

RONALD. I know you just started. I'd love to see how you work. The steps. I've never really seen a stonecutter's work in progress.

GENICE. It's not much to look at. You won't even be able to make out the features.

RONALD. I know. I'm just curious. Unless it would disturb your…Gregory.

(beat)

GENICE. No, it won't disturb him. He'll be fast asleep in the bedroom. We'll have to be quick though. I have to wake up early.

RONALD. Understood.

(Lights switch. Back with ABIGAIL. She sits on one end of the couch, drinking wine and smoking a cigarette. Keys in the door. RONALD enters.)

You're smoking.

ABIGAIL. You're observant. Did she have a former fiancé or not?

RONALD. He was sleeping.

ABIGAIL. Did you see him sleeping?

RONALD. He was in the bedroom.

ABIGAIL. Did you see anything that would lead you to believe he existed?

RONALD. Yes. Shoes. A leather jacket.

ABIGAIL. Not hers.

RONALD. Very large shoes. Boots. He exists.

ABIGAIL. All right.

(*She puts out the cigarette.*)

Did you see the gargoyle?

RONALD. Sort of. It's just the shape of it very loosely. You can sort of see a head.

ABIGAIL. Does it have wings? Is it like a demon?

RONALD. Not exactly. She's making it into a combination of a gargoyle and something else.

ABIGAIL. What's the something else?

RONALD. (*hesitates, then*) A Green Man.

ABIGAIL. What?

RONALD. A Green Man. You heard me.

ABIGAIL. Did you say that to be cruel?

RONALD. God, no, Abby. Jesus Christ, do you think I would say that to be cruel.

ABIGAIL. Why did you say…

RONALD. Because that's what it's called! It's a mythical creature from England or Ireland. A forest spirit. A good spirit. She wants to make a kind of good luck gargoyle.

(**ABIGAIL** *breaks and sobs.* **RONALD** *goes to her, holds her.*)

Abby, Abby…

It shocked me when she said it, too. It's like we're being forced to…

(She pulls herself up from him.)

ABIGAIL. Don't.

RONALD. Don't you think it's kind of significant?

ABIGAIL. I think you set it up to be. Bringing her on to your project. You went looking for it.

RONALD. I had the idea long before. It just happened now.

ABIGAIL. We both do it. It's sick.

RONALD. Do what?

ABIGAIL. Dwell. In this dwelling. In this hell. Punishing ourselves. Right?

RONALD. No, that's not what this is.

ABIGAIL. What do you call it?

RONALD. An accident.

ABIGAIL. It was our fault!

RONALD. Stop.

(Beat. She shifts gears.)

ABIGAIL. All right.

Is she a good kisser?

RONALD. What?

ABIGAIL. Genice. When you kissed.

RONALD. We didn't – You're drunk.

ABIGAIL. We're all drunk. That's the excuse. I wanted you to kiss her. That's why I sent you home with her. I wanted to see if you would. Maybe it'll make you more virile.

RONALD. It's time for bed.

ABIGAIL. Don't ignore me.

RONALD. There was no kissing.

*(**RONALD** gets up and exits.)*

ABIGAIL. You just went straight to sex, was that it? Is that what happened, Ronald?

*(**ABIGAIL** staggers off after **RONALD**. Lights switch. **GENICE** and **GREEN MAN** as **GREGORY** are lying naked against the evolving gargoyle. **GENICE** holds **GREGORY***

from behind, her arms and legs wrapped around him.
He sings a capella.)

GREGORY.

HOW LIKE THE WIND TO PLAY TRICKS WITH THE SOUNDS
   OF THE NIGHT
IN THE GARDEN
YOU WERE RIGHT
I WAS ONLY STARTING.

(Fade to black.)

ACT TWO

Scene One

(Morning. The sun is rising on **GENICE** *as she sculpts. Progress has been made.* **GREGORY** *sneaks on with a cup of coffee for her and one for him.)*

GREGORY. Lookin' good, honey.

(She jumps and shouts, startled.)

GENICE. You scared the crap out of me. I didn't hear you get up.

GREGORY. You've been working. You stop listening to the world around you when you're working. Coffee?

(She sets down her hammer and takes the coffee.)

It looks like you'll be done soon, huh?

GENICE. No, not for a while. What do you have today?

GREGORY. Wedding gig.

GENICE. Oh right. Bring some cake home for me.

GREGORY. I'll probably be late.

GENICE. It's supposed to rain tonight. You have to be careful.

GREGORY. Yes, ma'am.

GENICE. I worry about you.

GREGORY. I know. I like it.

GENICE. Get out of here, you big jerk, let me work.

GREGORY. *(bowing)* As you wish, your highness.

(He exits. Lights go to **ABIGAIL** *and* **RONALD**. **ABIGAIL** *is in her bathrobe, straightening* **RONALD**'s *tie. He holds a coffee.)*

ABIGAIL. Someday you'll learn how to tie a tie.

RONALD. What would I do without you?

ABIGAIL. Don't ask.

RONALD. What are you going to do today?

ABIGAIL. Try to work.

RONALD. Yeah?

ABIGAIL. Sure, why not, everyone else is doing it.

RONALD. I was thinking – and don't get mad at me – Maybe you should give Joyce a call. You know, because she asked Genice about you so she's interested in what you're up to.

ABIGAIL. But I'm not up to anything.

RONALD. No, I know, but it couldn't hurt to just keep the contact. And you have been working some. You said…

ABIGAIL. Nothing to show.

RONALD. Okay, I was just making a suggestion.

ABIGAIL. I never liked Joyce.

RONALD. Well, that's great Abigail, as you long as you keep up the positive attitude…

ABIGAIL. Thanks for the suggestion.

RONALD. I'm just trying to help. I'm always trying to help you.

Are you going to be okay today?

ABIGAIL. Yes, your emotionally unstable wife will be just fine.

RONALD. I didn't mean –

ABIGAIL. Are you going to be okay?

RONALD. Yeah. I'll call you at lunch.

ABIGAIL. I'll be here.

(He kisses her goodbye.)

RONALD. Good luck.

ABIGAIL. Good luck?

RONALD. With the work. Jesus, forget it. Have a good day. I love you.

(He kisses her again and she sees him out the door. **ABIGAIL** *is alone. She goes to her easel where her coffee waits. She drinks. She starts painting. Lights go to* **GENICE** *at the same time. She chisels. They both stop at the same time and sing a long held out note in the middle of their ranges – sort of like a long sigh, but not in defeat, in preparation… They both begin work again in silence. They stop. They breathe, their breaths in and out together. They return to work. They both stop.)*

ABIGAIL/GENICE. I see you in there.

(Lights fall on them and go to an isolated square spot, where **RONALD** *has just entered an implied elevator. DING!* **RONALD** *looks up at the passing floors above the implied elevator door.* **GARY** *slips into the elevator, definitely not through the door – he's just suddenly there. Silence.)*

GARY. Another day, another dollar.

*(***RONALD*** shouts in shock.)*

RONALD. Jesus, Gary, you scared the crap out of me.

GARY. Looks like you've got a lot on your mind.

RONALD. I suppose I do.

GARY. Busy day?

RONALD. Hm? No. Maybe. Want to go out to lunch?

(DING! Lights fall on them. Return to **ABIGAIL** *and* **GENICE**, *still working.* **GENICE** *stops, puts down her hammer. Time for a break. Exits.* **ABIGAIL** *stops, puts down her brush. Gets her phone. Practices before she puts it to her ear.)*

ABIGAIL. Hello, Joyce, it's Abigail. I wanted to talk to you.

–No, stupid, needy.

Hello, Joyce, I heard you were friends with Genice and Genice said you wanted to talk.

–No she didn't. She doesn't have any desire to talk to me, she just felt sorry for me.

ABIGAIL. *(cont.)*

Joyce, hello, it's Abigail Johanson, I heard you felt sorry for me so I'm here to cash in on it. And by the way, you did a terrible job promoting my last show.

–As long as you're positive, Abigail.

As long as you're positive.

Fuck it.

(She dials for real.)

Joyce, hi, it's Abigail. Abigail Johanson. I'm fine, how are you? I met a friend of yours recently. Genice. She's a stone sculptor. She's working on Ronald's new building. My husband.

I called because I'm working on something new. A series. I wanted to talk to you about it if you… Gargoyles.

Joyce, are you there?

(Lights switch to **RONALD** *and* **GARY** *playing racquetball. They are sweaty and mid-game, talking while they play.* **RONALD***'s getting his ass kicked.)*

RONALD. Jesus, what aren't you good at?

GARY. Holding on to girlfriends.

RONALD. Oh no, not again.

GARY. Yep, another one left me.

RONALD. For another guy?

GARY. Girl. She figured out she liked girls.

RONALD. Oh man. That happened to me once. Don't sweat it. It's not because of you. Probably.

GARY. Thanks.

RONALD. Listen, when you decide to get serious you'll find someone. But, Christ, why get serious now? Have fun, date lesbians, do whatever.

GARY. How did you meet your wife?

RONALD. Greece. We were looking at the same ruins.

GARY. Was it love at first sight?

(**RONALD** *stops.*)

RONALD. Yes, actually. It was like I saw someone I'd known all my life. Someone so familiar. I knew exactly how to talk to her; I didn't have to think about anything. It just happened. Like someone else was in control.

GARY. Some higher power…

RONALD. Something. Something beyond both of us. It was like we had no choice. We had to come together.

GARY. Is it still like that?

(**RONALD** *takes off his headband, game over.*)

RONALD. Yeah, of course.

(**GARY** *looks at him.*)

No. Now it feels like there's some force pushing us apart. Now it's something we have to fight through to stay together at all. That's the problem with saying anything's meant to be, Gary. If anything goes wrong, you have to assume that was meant to be, too. And, if that's true, then there's no point in fighting through anything. You have to start all over. You have to decide it's worth it, even if it was never meant to be to begin with.

(*A doorbell. Lights switch back to* **ABIGAIL**. *She's answering her door.* **GENICE**.)

GENICE. Hi. I think I might have left my wallet here. I've looked everywhere else.

ABIGAIL. I was wondering when you'd come.

GENICE. I think I left it in your bathroom.

ABIGAIL. Yes, you did. Hold on.

(*She goes off.* **GENICE** *looks around, sees a canvas, and takes a quick peek at it. Turns away from it just in time.* **ABIGAIL** *returns with the wallet.*)

Ronald says your gargoyle's coming along.

GENICE. Slowly but surely. Have you been painting?

ABIGAIL. A little. Yes.

GENICE. You got inspired?

ABIGAIL. You could say that.

(handing her the wallet)

I saw his picture. You left it open on the sink. That is him, isn't it? The guy. Your fiancé?

GENICE. Yes.

ABIGAIL. Must be an old picture. He looks very young.

GENICE. Did I come at a bad time?

ABIGAIL. Not at all. Why?

GENICE. You just seem a little…

ABIGAIL. Did you have sex with my husband?

GENICE. What?

ABIGAIL. You heard me.

GENICE. No. Jesus, Abby. I'll try to forget you said that.

*(She turns to go. **ABIGAIL** gets wilder and wilder.)*

ABIGAIL. Wait. Don't go. I apologize. I just had to ask. He's impotent with me so I wonder if he isn't with someone else. Do you want to see a painting?

GENICE. You just accused me of sleeping with your husband.

ABIGAIL. Yes.

GENICE. Why would you even think I would –

ABIGAIL. Who cares? I've moved on. Look.

(She shows her the very painting she had been peeking at.)

GENICE. You're a good painter.

ABIGAIL. It's a gargoyle.

GENICE. I see.

ABIGAIL. I haven't had sex for almost a year.

GENICE. Oh?

ABIGAIL. I'm acting crazy, aren't I?

GENICE. It's okay.

ABIGAIL. What really happened to your fiancé?

(**GENICE** *is silent.*)

All right, when was the last time *you* had sex?

GENICE. I think I'd better go.

ABIGAIL. That's what I thought. That's a long time.

GENICE. You aren't going to hurt yourself if I leave, are you?

ABIGAIL. I can't imagine how I could.

GENICE. I am very impressed by your work. I can't wait to see more later.

ABIGAIL. Likewise, I'm sure.

GENICE. Good-bye, Abigail.

ABIGAIL. *(grabbing her, but strangely calm)* Please don't leave me.

I took too many pills. I'm all scrambled. I can't see straight, I can't think.

GENICE. How many pills?

ABIGAIL. Just enough.

GENICE. Where's your phone?

ABIGAIL. What for?

GENICE. I'm calling 911.

ABIGAIL. No, I don't need that.

GENICE. How many pills did you take? The whole bottle?

ABIGAIL. A handful. My fingers are numb. My ears.

GENICE. Where's your phone?!

ABIGAIL. Bedroom.

(**GENICE** *runs off.* **ABIGAIL** *sinks to her knees. Lights switch to* **RONALD** *alone in the locker room, gym bag at his feet. He is almost dressed for work. His cell phone rings.*)

RONALD. Hello?

(**GENICE** *appears.*)

GENICE. Ronald, it's Genice. Your wife…

RONALD. Genice?

GENICE. No time. Look: I happened to be at your house. Your wife took too many pills. They're picking her up.

RONALD. What, what? Who?

GENICE. Ambulance. They're taking her to the hospital.

RONALD. Oh God, oh my God – is she awake, is she, tell me everything…

GENICE. She's passed out, they had to do CPR. She's breathing again. They're going to pump her stomach.

RONALD. Oh God oh God please no, not this –

GENICE. She'll be okay.

RONALD. You're just saying that.

GENICE. It'll be okay. Just come. Quickly.

(Blackout.)

Scene Two

(A hospital bed downstage. ABIGAIL lies on it, awake. GREEN MAN, dressed as a male nurse, is at the foot of her bed. They calmly look at each other.)

ABIGAIL. You work here, too?

GREEN MAN. Just got the job.

You almost died.

ABIGAIL. Would've served me right.

GREEN MAN. Why?

ABIGAIL. Making those paintings. It was wrong. And then I tried to show them. Like a monster. It was so wrong.

GREEN MAN. I hear your husband coming.

(He disappears. RONALD enters. Silence between them. He goes to her and puts his head on her chest, holding her tightly.)

ABIGAIL. You're crushing me, Ronald. What are you trying to do, kill me?

RONALD. That's not funny.

ABIGAIL. Sure it is.

RONALD. How do you feel?

ABIGAIL. Great. Ever had your stomach pumped? I highly recommend it.

RONALD. This really is not funny.

ABIGAIL. Who's laughing?

RONALD. I thought you were gone. When Genice called me I thought you were gone.

ABIGAIL. You'd be better off.

RONALD. Don't say that!

ABIGAIL. Why not, it's true. All we do is remind each other of what we lost.

RONALD. That's not all, we still have us.

ABIGAIL. Us. What a treat that is! I'm a basket case and you've got your head up your ass most of the time. What good are we to each other?

RONALD. We're husband and wife. That's what we are.

ABIGAIL. Listen to yourself. You barely believe it. Husband and wife means nothing to either of us.

RONALD. What are you saying?

ABIGAIL. You know what I'm saying. This isn't working. We're not going anywhere like this.

When I get out of here, I want to move in with my sister.

RONALD. What – you're what?

ABIGAIL. I have to get away from here. I have to get away from you. For both our sakes.

RONALD. We can work through this.

ABIGAIL. I don't think we can, Ronald. We've tried. Look at me. This is how I've been working through this. Everything has to change.

RONALD. Okay, I'll quit my job, go with you. We'll start again in a new town. We can change together.

ABIGAIL. We need to be separated.

RONALD. No.

ABIGAIL. No?

RONALD. I need you. I can't live without you.

ABIGAIL. Ronald…

RONALD. Please. I love you. I can't lose you.

I love you so much.

(He's on his knees beside her now. Silence.)

ABIGAIL. Did you see my paintings?

RONALD. Your paintings?

ABIGAIL. Go home and look at them. Tell me it's helping us in any way to stay together. Look at the hideous faces on them. Tell me there's anything worth keeping here.

RONALD. Where are you? Where's my Abby?

ABIGAIL. Gone. Lost. She flew out the window.

*(He stares at her. Kisses her head. He has to get out of the room – he leaves. **GREEN MAN** re-enters.)*

GREEN MAN. He's devoted to you.

ABIGAIL. Hopelessly.

GREEN MAN. Do you think you can live without him?

ABIGAIL. I used to live without him. There was a time when I never knew he existed. I had a life to myself. Did only what I wanted. Never had so much invested in anyone but me. Only ever had myself to blame for the things that went wrong.

GREEN MAN. And now?

ABIGAIL. I blame both of us.

(**GREEN MAN** *wheels her bed off. Lights go to* **GENICE**, *standing with* **RONALD** *in the hospital lobby.*)

GENICE. How is she?

RONALD. Terrible. Thank you for waiting.

GENICE. They're keeping her here?

RONALD. She's done this before.

GENICE. With pills?

RONALD. With the oven.

GENICE. Jesus.

How are you?

RONALD. I don't even know. I gotta get out of here.

GENICE. Not back to work.

RONALD. I don't want to go home.

GENICE. Come to my place.

RONALD. I don't know.

GENICE. I'll make you some food.

RONALD. What about Gregory?

GENICE. Out of town gig.

(*Pause. He looks at her.*)

RONALD. All right.

(*Lights go to* **GREGORY**, *with a guitar. He sings.*)

(*Music: "The Stars"*)

GREGORY.

    THE STARS ARE LIKE JEWELS IN THE NIGHT
    WATCHING OUR MOVES
    FROM THEIR DIZZYING HEIGHTS
    HOW LIKE THE VAST EMPTY SPACE
    THERE BETWEEN YOU AND ME IN THIS PLACE

    (**RONALD** *and* **GENICE** *enter, slow-dancing in a melancholy way.*)

    LOVE IS A MYSTERY TO ME
    HIGHER ABOVE
    ANYTHING I CAN SEE
    IT'S AS WIDE AS THE INFINITE SEA
    YOU ARE THE TIDE I DIVE BENEATH

    AND THE MOON GOES DOWN
    AND THE ONLY LIGHT AROUND
    IS FROM THE LIGHTNING
    FORKED ACROSS THE SKY
    SCORCHED ACROSS YOUR EYES

    THE STARS ARE LIKE EYES IN THE NIGHT
    WATCHING OUR MOVES
    FROM THEIR DIZZYING HEIGHTS
    HOW LIKE THE VAST EMPTY SPACE
    THERE BETWEEN YOU AND ME IN THIS PLACE

    (*He exits.* **RONALD** *and* **GENICE** *pull away from each other.*)

RONALD. Did he write that for you?

GENICE. Yes.

RONALD. It's a nice recording.

GENICE. I'm glad you like it.

RONALD. When did he write it?

GENICE. Shortly after we got engaged. We were apart a lot. He always had these gigs.

RONALD. Like now.

GENICE. Like now.

RONALD. He has a nice voice. It's good to hear it.

GENICE. Yes, it is.

RONALD. I should go back to the hospital.

GENICE. Of course.

RONALD. Thank you for feeding me. And the wine.

GENICE. Are you okay to drive?

RONALD. Probably.

(staggers a little)

Maybe not. But I can't just leave her there.

GENICE. I'll make you some coffee.

RONALD. No, don't. I'll be fine. I just need a couple minutes to rest.

(He sits on the floor. She sits with him.)

GENICE. You're a good dancer.

RONALD. Abigail thinks we're having an affair.

GENICE. I know.

RONALD. Are we?

GENICE. I don't think one slow dance constitutes an affair, do you?

RONALD. Abby thinks he doesn't live with you anymore.

GENICE. She said.

RONALD. Does he?

GENICE. Less and less.

(He looks at her.)

I do find you very attractive.

RONALD. I can't…

GENICE. I know. I just wanted you to know. I shouldn't have said anything.

RONALD. No, it's fine. I find you attractive, too. I mean, I can't, even if I wanted to.

I better hit the road.

GENICE. Okay.

(They pause. He stands.)

RONALD. Thank you for everything. With Abigail. You saved her.

GENICE. I was there at the right time.

(She stands. They kiss good-bye, sweetly and quickly, like friends.)

Drive safely.

(He smiles and leaves. Silence. **GREGORY** *enters.)*

GREGORY. Who was that leaving?

GENICE. Ronald. His wife tried to kill herself.

How was your gig?

GREGORY. It was good. Getting back was a pain. All that rain out there.

(She touches his shirt.)

GENICE. You're all wet. We need to get you out of these clothes.

GREGORY. If you insist.

(She leads him off. Lights go to **ABIGAIL** *in her hospital bed. Sitting up on the phone.)*

ABIGAIL. Delores, it's me. Oh, I'm okay. You?

Listen, I'm calling because I wanted to ask you if I could come stay with you. No, just me. Well, I don't know, a couple weeks, maybe more. I might want to move back. No, just me. Yes. I think Ronald and I… Don't start crying. Please, Delores, this is hard enough. I'm just asking if I can… Goddamit, stop crying!

Can I come stay with you?

(The lights shift to **RONALD** *and* **ABIGAIL***'s place. A key in the door, then* **RONALD** *enters, alone. He looks around the place, sits on the couch. He talks as if* **GARY** *were with him. It becomes obvious that he's drunk.)*

RONALD. The truth is, Gary, my wife keeps trying to kill herself. The truth is, I've lost my lust for architecture. The truth is: you get older and shit happens that fucks you up. And then you die. But you're supposed to be grateful if along the way you found love, or purpose, or ever had something happen to you that felt like a miracle. Even if you live to see it all torn away from you. What do you think of that, Gary? Am I still your hero? When I die no one will remember my name like Louis Sullivan's. When I die, the love of my life will not be with me anymore. When I die, I will have no son to… I have no son.

(**RONALD** *stands and goes to the window, leans out it a little.*)

Hello, Green Man.

(**RONALD** *starts to topple out, he stops himself and throws his body away from the window, sick and out of control, falling to the floor.*)

I miss you, Abby. I feel very lonely here. I feel…

(*He sees something – the paintings. He stumbles to them, looks at them. One by one. He cries all over them. Lights fall.*)

Scene Three

(Lights rise on **GENICE**, *draped asleep over her gargoyle. Morning.* **GREGORY** *enters in a bathrobe, with his morning cup of coffee. He's playing out the exact same scene as at the top of the act, regardless of what she says.)*

GREGORY. Lookin' good, honey.

*(***GENICE*** blinks her eyes awake.)*

GENICE. Gregory?

GREGORY. You've been working. You stop listening to the world when you're working.

Coffee?

(He offers her his cup. She takes it and drinks.)

It looks like you'll be done soon, huh?

GENICE. Almost.

(He looks at her expectantly, like he's waiting for a line. She reluctantly gives in.)

What do you have to do today?

GREGORY. Wedding gig.

GENICE. Wedding. Of course it's a wedding gig.

GREGORY. I'll probably be late.

GENICE. Why don't you skip it.

(He smiles at her with a tinge of sadness. Again she gives in.)

It's supposed to rain tonight.

Be careful.

GREGORY. Yes, ma'am.

GENICE. I love you, Gregory. I miss you.

GREGORY. I know. I like it.

GENICE. Can I have a kiss?

GREGORY. As you wish, your highness.

(She goes to him. They kiss. He exits. She drinks her coffee, alone. Lights go to **RONALD** *on the phone, in his office.)*

RONALD. Neil, please don't do this. Yes, I'm begging you. Because she's already started working. She's started carving the stone. Because I saw it. Fuck expenses, we're not going bankrupt, you're just being cheap because you don't like the idea. I'll use whatever tone of voice I want, you're not my boss. Are you threatening me? Don't do this.

When?

You bastard. She was counting on this job. Contract or no, she started because it looked like it was a done deal. She was excited, she's an artist.

(trying another tactic)

She could sue us, Neil. Yes, she could. Verbal contract. I'll back her up.

What are you gonna do about it? Yes, I am threatening you. Well, you just try to do that. I'm one of the best architects here. This is going to cost you your job, not mine.

(He hangs up, with righteous indignation.)

Shit.

(He dials a number. **GENICE** *enters, in a bathrobe, on the phone, pressing a hot water bottle to her head.)*

GENICE. Hello?

RONALD. Hi, it's Ronald.

GENICE. Oh, hi.

RONALD. I, uh, just wanted to thank you again for last night.

GENICE. Of course. How's Abigail?

RONALD. Back home. They let her go this morning.

She might be leaving me. She's deciding.

GENICE. Leaving you?

RONALD. Yeah. I can't even think about that right now. I called you about something else.

Some stuff being tossed around here. Thoughts people are having about the gargoyles. I need to get out of the office. Can I come over and talk to you?

GENICE. Am I being fired?

RONALD. No, of course not. I just want to talk in person.

GENICE. It sounds like I'm being fired.

RONALD. Not by me. You should have gotten a written contract. But, look, nothing's done yet. Can I come over?

GENICE. You're hitting me with a lot at once here, Ronald.

RONALD. I know. We'll work it out.

GENICE. My job or your wife leaving you?

RONALD. I want to talk to you face-to-face.

GENICE. Okay.

Can you give my hangover an hour before you show up?

RONALD. Of course.

GENICE. See you soon.

(She hangs up. So does he. He thinks a moment, dials another number. **ABIGAIL** *enters, also in a bathrobe.)*

ABIGAIL. Hello?

*(***RONALD*** is silent. He hangs up. So does she. He puts on his jacket and exits.* **ABIGAIL** *puts down the phone and goes to her easel, which has been set up between scenes. A blank canvas is on it. She stares at it. A doorbell sounds.* **ABIGAIL** *opens the door. The* **GREEN MAN** *enters, wearing the same bathrobe as when he was* **GREGORY.** *He stands before her. He starts to take off his robe, she stops him.)*

I just want to paint your face.

GREEN MAN. I thought you didn't need my face.

ABIGAIL. I changed my mind. Sit there.

*(He sits on the couch. **ABIGAIL** goes to her easel.)*

GREEN MAN. How do you want me to look at you?

ABIGAIL. Just hold still.

*(Lights go to **GENICE**'s, but don't leave **ABIGAIL** as she starts painting. **GENICE** and **RONALD** at her door.)*

RONALD. Did I give you enough time?

GENICE. Yes, come in.

RONALD. Is Gregory home?

GENICE. He's playing for an event all day.

RONALD. What a life.

GENICE. It's not exactly what he'd like to be doing. It's not his music.

RONALD. *(moving in, looking at the sculpture)* You really have been making some progress. You work quickly.

GENICE. So what are we talking about here?

RONALD. My boss's evil underling is trying to get you off the project.

I'm doing everything I can to keep you.

If for some reason I can't, I think you have grounds for a lawsuit. I'll support you.

GENICE. Forget it.

RONALD. Why? It's not fair. There was a verbal contract.

GENICE. Between you and me. I'd be suing you.

RONALD. You'd be suing the company. I'd be vouching for the company's part of the deal.

GENICE. Forget it.

RONALD. I don't want you to get screwed over.

GENICE. If it doesn't end up being for the building, then it'll just be for me. That's fine.

RONALD. It's not fine. I'm sick of bullshit like this.

GENICE. It's the way of the world.

Do you want a drink?

RONALD. No. All right.

GENICE. Make yourself comfortable.

(*She exits. He sits.*)

GREEN MAN. What do you see in my face?

ABIGAIL. Goodness. Kindness. Someone I've always imagined.

GREEN MAN. Who?

ABIGAIL. Someone who calls to you and you go to him.

GREEN MAN. Like a friend?

ABIGAIL. In a way.

GREEN MAN. A lover?

ABIGAIL. No.

GREEN MAN. Who then?

(*Silence.* **RONALD** *looks at the sculpture.*)

RONALD. You can make out his face now.

Is it modeled after anyone?

(**GENICE** *enters with drinks and a photo in a frame. She gives a drink and the photo to him. He holds it. Looks from it to the statue.*)

Your fiancé?

GENICE. Yes.

RONALD. He looks like he's twenty.

GENICE. Twenty-four.

RONALD. He's a good-looking guy.

GENICE. Yes, he was.

(*He looks at the picture and the sculpture.*)

RONALD. How did he die?

(*pause*)

GENICE. On the way back from a gig.

It was raining. He ran into a tree.

GREEN MAN. What do you see when you look at me?

ABIGAIL. The Green Man. I see the green man.

RONALD. He's still here with you. You still see him…

GENICE. He comes and goes. He came again when I met you and Abby.

ABIGAIL. Green man. I hear his voice when I look at you.

RONALD. The Green Man.

GENICE. That means something to you that it doesn't to me, doesn't it.

RONALD. It was the last thing he said.

GENICE. Who? Oh.

Do you want to –

RONALD. We heard him from the other room.

ABIGAIL. Green man.

GENICE. Your child? He said –

RONALD. I had just come home from work.

ABIGAIL. I was painting. He was in his crib with the crayons and the paper.

RONALD. I came in and swept her up in my arms and took her to the bedroom.

ABIGAIL. He threw me on the bed and I was laughing. We were kissing, rolling around.

RONALD/ABIGAIL. We were so happy.

RONALD. And from the living room we heard him:

ABIGAIL. "Green man."

RONALD. His little voice.

ABIGAIL. Ronald said:

RONALD. "Who's the green man?"

ABIGAIL. Shouted out while he was lying on top of me.

RONALD. He kept shouting it over and over again like children do when they find something they like to say.

ABIGAIL. Green man, green man, green man!

RONALD. And then we started saying it: Green man, green man, green man!

ABIGAIL. And then all the sudden it stopped.

Ronald. Ronald!

RONALD. We both ran out to the living room.

ABIGAIL. And he was gone.

RONALD. He wasn't in the crib.

ABIGAIL. He never climbed out, he couldn't have climbed out.

RONALD. The window was open.

ABIGAIL. I had left the window open.

RONALD. We ran to the window.

Right below our building there's a green figure sticking out. A gargoyle. Is it a gargoyle? It's not on a roof, it just juts out from our building under our window.

ABIGAIL. His arms outstretched, reaching.

RONALD. Like he was reaching for him but he couldn't hold him.

ABIGAIL. The green man.

RONALD. He fell right through his arms.

That was the green man.

ABIGAIL. If I had closed the window.

RONALD. If I hadn't taken her into the bedroom.

ABIGAIL. If we had gone to see who the green man was before…

RONALD. Gary would still be…

GENICE. Gary.

RONALD. Our son. We didn't understand. And then he was gone. And it's our fault.

GENICE. No.

ABIGAIL. I want to think there was something else. Someone else.

RONALD. There's no one else to blame.

ABIGAIL. *(to* **GREEN MAN***)* Like you.

RONALD. Just us.

ABIGAIL. *(to* **GREEN MAN***)* I need to think it was someone like you.

(silence)

RONALD. *(directly to* **GENICE***)* How do I stop thinking like that?

ABIGAIL. *(to* **GREEN MAN***)* How will I ever stop needing you?

GENICE. You won't. You'll never stop.

(The **GREEN MAN** *gets up and walks away.)*

You just learn to live life at the same time.

ABIGAIL. And then you're gone. Where do you go?

(Dark on **ABIGAIL***.)*

GENICE. Are you okay?

RONALD. Yeah. No.

GENICE. You should go home. You should go home to your wife.

RONALD. Will you be okay?

GENICE. I'm used to this.

Go.

*(***RONALD** *turns and exits.* **GENICE** *picks up her hammer. Dark on her.)*

Scene Four

(Lights go to **ABIGAIL** *and* **RONALD***'s house.* **RONALD**
has just walked in.)

ABIGAIL. Hi.

RONALD. Hi.

ABIGAIL. You're home early. Did you forget something?

RONALD. No.

ABIGAIL. You came to make sure I was still alive.

RONALD. Yes.

Have you been painting?

ABIGAIL. Yeah, a little.

RONALD. I looked at your gargoyles last night.

ABIGAIL. What did you think?

RONALD. I think you're very brave.

ABIGAIL. Brave?

RONALD. To face it. To paint it.

ABIGAIL. I haven't been able to paint anything else.

I hate it.

RONALD. Is this another one?

(She's silent. She very simply turns the painting to him.)

It's different. The face. It's…kind.

ABIGAIL. Do you know what tomorrow is?

RONALD. I don't even know what today is. What's to –

(It rushes to him.)

Yes.

I know.

(pause)

ABIGAIL. I dreamt about him last night.

RONALD. Did you?

ABIGAIL. He was a baby.

RONALD. In your dream?

ABIGAIL. I was watching you hold him.

He fit between your hand and your elbow.

You were so gentle with him, careful.

And then he was older. He was growing.

You held his hand, him standing beside you. Looking up at you.

I liked watching you with him.

RONALD. I loved watching you.

(Silence. Deciding to connect to it more, connecting with **RONALD.***)*

ABIGAIL. Cutting his hair.

RONALD. *(same)* Putting on his shoes.

ABIGAIL. Changing his diapers.

RONALD. Giving him a bath.

Him splashing around, laughing.

ABIGAIL. His teeth coming in.

RONALD. Crying in the middle of the night. All night.

You feeding him.

ABIGAIL. Holding him, rocking him.

RONALD. Him sleeping between us. Us looking down at him. Looking at each other. So happy.

(They look at each other.)

ABIGAIL. You were such a good father.

RONALD. You were such a wonderful mother.

ABIGAIL. I can't ever forgive us.

RONALD. I don't want to.

ABIGAIL. I want to remember him.

RONALD. Can we now?

(She nods. They go to each other. Silence.)

ABIGAIL. I've been watching myself. Watching how I act, not believing it's me. Feeling like I'm acting something out that's not true. Not knowing how to act at all.

And then you come home and I don't know how to be with you.

RONALD. Do you still want to be with me?

ABIGAIL. You're hardly there. I miss you like I miss him.

RONALD. I'm right here. I'm here now.

ABIGAIL. I feel you. It's been a while.

(They take each other in.)

RONALD. Am I going to lose you?

ABIGAIL. You haven't yet.

RONALD. What about everything you said?

ABIGAIL. I'm still here.

Aren't I?

*(**RONALD** nods. Silence. She kisses him.)*

We're still here.

Scene Five

(GENICE's. RONALD and ABIGAIL stand before her, having just come in. RONALD is holding a cake box. The statue is completely covered with a drop cloth.)

GENICE. Come in, come in.

Let me take your coats.

Please. Sit down.

(She goes to hang the coats.)

I'm so glad you're here.

ABIGAIL. Thank you for having us.

GENICE. Of course. It's been a while since I've had… company.

I bought some wine.

I have some candles. When you said there was a cake. I bought some candles.

(She produces them, little birthday candles.)

Are these okay?

RONALD. Perfect.

GENICE. So shall we…

(They all sit. RONALD puts the cake down. GENICE gives RONALD the candles. He opens the candle box.)

RONALD. One for each?

GENICE. One for each?

ABIGAIL. Three.

GENICE. Oh, yes. Of course.

Three.

How do you want to – Do you want to say anything?

ABIGAIL. No. Unless you do.

GENICE. Me?

RONALD. For yours.

GENICE. No.

(GENICE *holds out her hand for a candle.* **RONALD** *hands her one, takes one and gives one to* **ABIGAIL**. **ABIGAIL** *lights them with her lighter. They all put their candles in the cake together. Silence.*)

GENICE. I love the way flame moves. Like a dancer. So strong and graceful.

ABIGAIL. So delicate.

RONALD. So alive.

(*Silence.* **ABIGAIL** *sits back in the sofa, sees the hidden sculpture.*)

ABIGAIL. Can we see it? What you've done.

GENICE. I didn't think you'd want to.

ABIGAIL. I do.

(**GENICE** *stands and goes to the sculpture under the cloth. She looks back.* **RONALD** *and* **ABIGAIL** *nod, the candles flicker.* **GENICE** *pulls the sheet away. The* **GREEN MAN** *is beneath, as the sculpture.*)

ABIGAIL. Are you finished with it?

GENICE. Almost.

ABIGAIL. (*to* **RONALD**) Will they let you use it?

RONALD. I don't know.

GENICE. It doesn't matter.

ABIGAIL. He's beautiful.

Is that really what he looked like?

GENICE. (*She looks at* **GREEN MAN**) Yes. This is how I see him now. This is how I remember him.

Is somebody going to blow out the candles?

(*The* **GREEN MAN** *blows. The candles go out. Silence.*)

ABIGAIL. Who wants cake?

(*Lights fall as they start to eat. End of play.*)